pieces of accordance.

by: liz rau

Printed by CreateSpace, An Amazon.com Company

Available on Kindle and other online stores

CreateSpace ISBN-13: 978-1540319241

CreateSpace ISBN-10: 1540319245

Edited by: Liz Rau & Sue Rau

Cover Design: Mathew Jennings – Blue Bamboo Creative

Information: LizRauInfo@gmail.com

follow liz rau on social media.

Website: www.LizRauOfficial.com

Facebook – Liz Rau Official

Twitter – @LizRauOfficial

Instagram – @LizRauOfficial

Official Book Hashtag - #PiecesByRau

other books by liz rau.

The Trials: Secrets, Spells and Tales

Spellbound: Secrets, Spells & Tales *(Coming 2017)*

dedication.

To Mom and Dad:
Thank you for allowing me to grow up as a
'High Street Rau'.

"Where so many hours have been spent in convincing myself that I am right, is there not some reason to fear I may be wrong?"

Jane Austen

table of contents.

prologue.

Tears cascaded down Eliza's cheeks from her deep brown chocolate eyes. The trunk had to go, she could no longer bear to look at it. There was hollowness where her heart once had been. Had it beaten just days ago with the thrill of true love? Now it only thumped with agony and sorrow.

Eliza glared at the trunk she'd traveled with from Missouri to New York. Had she truly believed she could take this with her? No. All reminders of the blissfully perfect, wonderful life she once lived needed to be removed from her line of vision. Physical pain exploded within her chest from just a mere thought of her past. How had this happened? How could fate be so cruel?

"Mama, no cry." Small, delicate fingers reached up to wipe the sadness away from Eliza's cold, pale cheeks.

"It's okay, baby girl. We're okay." Eliza tried her best attempt to soothe her daughter. "We're going to be happy again. England is beautiful."

Eliza prayed that was true. She traced her lace-gloved fingers over the small torn hole in the bright red lining of the trunk, as though she were saying one last goodbye to her family, and slammed the lid shut – locking away any last memory of the life she once had.

Eliza and baby Alma Jane would find happiness once more in their new life. The survival of her heart depended upon it. Eliza planned to take a one way passage across the Atlantic and would never be returning. At least, not in this lifetime.

chapter one.

The hardwood floors were creaking with every soft step taken. Only Sasha Reeds would find that particularly delicate sound to be a comfort in life. And the smell - there was nothing like the smell of an old house. Sasha swore she could whiff the faintest aromas of homemade apricot jam, brandy with the shadowy scent of cigar smoke, and even the slightest trace of cinnamon throughout the home. The glimmer of past familiarity offered a sense of the warm heart and jolly laughter that was once so prevalent throughout these walls. Rays of rainbow hues and prismatic light shined through the alcove windows thanks to the original stained glass images that were still intact. Three antique fireplaces still remained untouched on the first floor, each defining the dwelling with an engraved portrait depicting whether the space was a dining room, gentleman's parlor or a ladies sitting room.

Stepping through the corridor walks, Sasha noted how each hallway arched at every entrance, amiably greeting those who entered the music room or the foyer – where she could sense the ghost of a once glorious grand stairwell. Those who had lived in the house during year's past had left ornamental, sheet-covered furniture scattered throughout each room on the main level. She had been shocked and wonderstruck to discover most pieces were original – dated from the late 1800s to early 1900s. Each singular white sheet had a dusty layer threatening to fly in the air, likely to spiral like a breeze through the heavy wooden pocket doors that closed each room. For Sasha, this wasn't just any house - it was a house that spoke of a history, a story. Now, this storied house was her home.

The curbside appeal of the home was something similar to that of a dollhouse little girls could only dream of. So decoratively painted in shades of grays and blues, any soul walking the street would have to take note of how harmoniously the home sang to the gorgeously aged oak trees lining the street, and the flourishing dogwood shadowing the driveway. The blooms of the tree brought out the deep red accents on the porch spindles and above the main windows. The decorative touch added a smile to Sasha's eyes, as the color added just enough to the facade to echo the stained glass in the sunlight.

Set in stone, the basement was somewhat visible behind small garden beds on both sides of the porch. The stone reflected the antique edge to the home, and Sasha likened it to a dungeon type setting in her own thoughts – though it was nothing of the sort. The space was simply filled with too many cobwebs for her city tastes. The porch was absolutely gorgeous and she could see that at one time it had wrapped around the house, towards the dining room side of the home, where a rather huge pine tree stood. It was a tree so large that it had to be at least a hundred years old. Perhaps it had been there before the house?

Before there was a story here? Her thoughts became enraptured with theories of the history of the home. Were there secret passageways? Scandalous balls? Whiskey trading during the prohibition? Oh the tales the walls were sure to tell.

But what story, Sasha thought. *What happened here?*

With a realtor guiding her through the abandoned abode, Sasha found herself too eagerly curious to know those answers. Rumor had it that a simple saloon owner crafted the house - a Queen Anne Victorian - in the early 1880s. That man had married a high society Lady, and with that union came many responsibilities and expectations. The aesthetics of the saloon owner's design were beautifully articulated both on the interior and exterior. The landscaping area, for a potentially breath-taking garden in the extremely spacious backyard, was the setting for many-a-good conversation once manicured thoroughly.

Sasha was nervous about being in such a quiet town, so small and quaint. It was definitely a gem hidden in the middle-of-nowhere Missouri. But, more interesting to her, it was a town rich in history. It was that simple fact that added more allure to the house for Sasha. She was a writer, or at least attempting to become one. Throughout her life, ideas had never ceased to flow in and out of her mind in an endless stream of fascinating daydreams, but she had never been courageous enough to create anything on her own. Sasha told herself she had yet to be inspired enough to put ink to paper, let alone fingertips to a keyboard. In truth, though, she simply had no clue where to begin, and was terrified of what may happen when she finally chose a path. *What if she failed?*

Her grandmother's passing had somehow changed that notion within her, especially after her dearly departed parental figure had left her such a peculiar treasure. An antique traveling trunk from the 1904 World's Fair had been left to her, and the interest in this house began after seeing a photograph of it locked away within it. Sasha had never seen the photo before, not even in her childhood, but the image drew her focus into it so intently, she found herself mesmerized. Why had her grandmother kept an old black and white photograph of a house? It was taken sometime around the turn of the century. Within the image of the Victorian home, Sasha could make out a family on the porch, though their faces not clear, and a second couple on the left side of the house, swinging in the yard on what appeared to be a picture-perfect day. Sasha sensed a familiarity about the photo, but was unable to place it.

After a heavy amount of research into where the house was from, Sasha discovered the house was for sale. With her grandmother's inheritance of a highly significant sum, Sasha began to toy with the notion that she should follow the path that had now begun to consume her current whimsical fantasies. What would her grandmother do? Though the woman had not only been wealthy, and downright rich, she hadn't lived much above her means. No, her grandmother took out of life only what she truly needed: contentment. It was a quality Sasha admired.

Sasha knew that the big antique clunky trunk would not have been left to her on a whim, and the Will had confirmed such intuition when Sasha was read the following passage:

> **"People grow through experience if they meet life honestly and courageously. This is how character is built. My dear Sasha, do not forget**

to grow."

Sasha had pondered this note from her grandmother for months, sleeping with the image of the Queen Anne Victorian, depicting a day in the family's life, by her bed. Her grandmother had known of Sasha's seemingly never ending case of writer's block. Sasha had no idea where to begin a story, or why her grandmother kept the photo to begin with. But each night, she found her imagination creating faces and names of those in the photograph. She found herself wanting to know more and more about the past of the house.

Her grandmother was not a soul who kept *things*. Stuff was not kept by the woman at all really, outside of jewelery and a few family heirlooms. In her Will, Sasha's grandmother had left nearly all possessions to the Salvation Army - but not the bulky and beaten brown leather trunk with the 1904 World's Fair emblem; no, that had been left to Sasha along with the money.

No doubt was established within Sasha's thoughts as to whether or not the house had charm, as she was positive the home had been swimming in its allure since its contruction. The moment her eyes laid rest on the Queen Anne Victorian and all its beauty, Sasha knew she had not only found her home, she found a story. Every fiber within her body, along with her gut, reaffirmed she was supposed to be there. And with her mind on the ghost of a grand staircase, Sasha could practically feel the ball going on around her. Immersing herself completely into her inspiring daydreams, she recognized how magnetically tied to this home she had become, as if it owned her.

Stepping off the flight from New York, Sasha had already decided she would purchase the home. She had never sensed herself so unexpectedly peace before. Sasha wondered, though, why nobody had snatched the house up yet. The salesman told her it had been on the market for nearly five years, and that all previous owners never overstayed their welcome.

As far as Sasha Reeds was concerned, these walls had tales to tell. At last, she had found a place to start.

chapter two.

The sound of the horse hooves on cobblestone caused Charles to glance up from his workbench, drawing in the most anxious breath. The large coach was remarkable in its exquisite features of onyx siding with gold trimming and wonderful plush seating that comfortably sat four people on its shiny royal red leather interior. Charles let out his breath as the horses slowed the coach to a stop, allowing him to recognize the luscious brown curls piled neatly atop a very pretty head.

Dropping the blueprints, Charles brushed the dirt off of his hands against his legs, leaving light colored prints on his dark fitted trousers. As he made his way down the slope of the lawn to the lane to greet his visitors, out of the vehicle came Mrs. Williams, followed by the strapping young six-year-old Mr. Jakob Williams, and then lastly, Miss Williams. Charles had to wipe the sweat from his palms once more at the sight of his lovely Eliza. *Would she never cease to make him nervous?*

"Miss Eliza, how do you fare today?"

"Such a gentleman, you are, to always be distraught with concern over my well-being, Charles."

He held her hand moments longer than necessary as she allowed him to lift her down from the coach. Just the slightest intimacy of her touch thrilled him, and Eliza herself, he suspected. She blushed at the contact of his hand, and even through her laced glove he thought she could feel the calloused, hardened skin of his palms.

Eliza Williams was just shy of turning an enchanting eighteen-years-old, and had been affianced to Charles Hoffmeister for the past six months. The twosome were to be wed close to the Holiday, and Charles couldn't have been happier to see the first turn of the leaves that morning. The brilliance of red and orange hues colored the skyline of High Street. The change of season brought supreme ambiance to his mood, as he was one more season closer to a forever-blissful union. Eliza had charmed Charles from their first chance meeting on Main Street, right outside of his pub. Or was it technically inside his pub?

Young Mr. Jakob, Eliza's mischievous cute younger brother, had scampered off from his sister at the local grocer's market, and into his saloon, Scottie's Pub. Even though it was an all male club full of the town's finest gentlemen, drunks, gamblers and sinners that every woman hates, Eliza had rushed through the doors to pull Jakob out before he found himself in harms way. The moment she entered what was known as a gentlemen's sacred establishment, men crowded and the music faded, the room buzzing with excited interest and salacious drool. No woman had ever dared to enter a man's foxhole club, the place where the men came to escape from the 'little lady'. But Eliza had, and with defiant moxy all over her fine features, she appeared neither abashed nor fearful of it.

After sighting Jakob by the piano, trying to climb to the top of the instrument, Eliza promptly marched over to the corner of the pub, grabbed his hand, and tried to dash out the path she'd come. Charles could faintly hear the small woman scolding the boy about "*What mother is going to do...*"

Eliza had nearly reached the door when a sleazy drunkard stepped out into her path, purposely blockading the door, and vilely smelling as though his whole body had bathed in whiskey.

"Please move sir. The young one did not mean any offense with his intrusion". Eliza straightened her spine in an attempt to appear as tall as she could.

The drunkard was Mr. Thomas Pratt, notoriously vicious with his vulgar tongue-lashings of an embarrassing and most provocative nature. The man was on his third wife at the moment. Though both prior wives supposedly died of natural causes, it was always among the ever growing rumor mill that those wives, had indeed, given up their lives with a broken heart after never feeling love in their marriage.

"It isn't the young'n who's intruding, prissy. He is at least male. I am sure I can safely assumeeeee you are not," he slurred, intrusively letting his eyes roam all over her figure.

Charles saw his hand start to move for her hip and jolted towards them, placing himself in between the two. "Pratt! Leave the lady alone or I'll kindly remove your drunken arse out of my pub."

"She shouldn't be here Charlesssss," Pratt slurred. "Are you going to let them all come in now? Infest this place with lace and perfume? Are you going to start putting doilies on the table and using tea cups for our brandy? Start a knitting club?" Pratt stumbled his beer belly back to his losing streak at the poker table nearby, and hiccupped as he plopped down.

Charles gently placed a hand on Eliza's back, guiding her through the doorway out into the fresh air

14

and warm sunlight. He leaned down to the child, who now looked guilty as sin, and chuckled. "Keep your nose clean kid and you can come back when you're of age, alright?"

The boy grinned, a toothy smile so large it covered his whole face, but did not look up at his older sister, knowing punishment was still on its way. Charles chuckled once more.

"He'll be doing no such thing. Jakob's going to be a bestie, as honorable as his father and grandfather."

Charles then glanced up, really assessing her for the first time. He might as well have taken a punch to the chest from Pratt, for his heart sure was sore and his hands became unbearably damp. The lady had pearl white skin, which was deeply contrasted by her rich coffee hair curling around her pretty features, smoldering dark chocolate eyes and luscious apple lips. She was maybe only half a foot over five feet, short compared to his towering strong frame. Charles found her to be thin, but rounded with curves. As he caught himself staring into her eyes, he took in the slight trace of pink crossing her cheeks, which only made her prettier in her mint green day dress. Green was unusual for the young women in the area, who normally wore a variation of pink or lavender. Charles favored it though, as anything paler than a rose seemed wrong for her.

"Pardon my incorrigible manners Miss, thought it best to get you out of Scottie's before Mr. Pratt's liquor became verbal courage. My name is Charles Hoffmeister, proprietor of this establishment."

Fascinated, he became a silent audience as he watched Eliza curiously study him. He was handsome, devilishly so. Tall and muscularly solid, with ginger-bronzed red hair and not a single freckle across his features. His eyes were ice blue, mysteriously deep, and a shade unlike any she had ever seen.

"I'm Miss Eliza Williams. Jakob and I are certainly gracious, but certainly in a hurry. We beg your pardon, but please have a nice day."

With that the siblings turned, walking at a brisk pace, and Charles could hear poor, impish young Jakob being scolded as he observed them cross the road back to Pete's Market.

Charles remembered that day quite fondly, as did Eliza. From then on he wondered out on to the streets from his pub, simply hopeful, and sometimes desperate, to catch even a glimpse of her. She, in turn, began making more and more visits downtown, assisting him in catching a glance of her - and often times - a smile. These were memories cherished by Charles, as he realized those secret smiles were the start to his life.

Mrs. Williams made a small coughing sound then,

signaling the twosome to disengage their hands. The couple had been frozen in time on the carriage step still, and had been so close Eliza could have inhaled in his salted-sweaty scent from building their home.

"Where is Mr. Williams then? Working on a Saturday?" Charles inquired as he linked arms with the ladies, guiding them up the path from the cobblestone lane, reluctantly jumping out of his daydream.

"Elijah stated he'd be calling on you later to check the progress of the house. He has appointments this morning and very well could not be torn away," Mrs. Williams answered. Mrs. Williams was not but nine and thirty, very beautiful and still in her prime. She held a grace and elegance that was common for a woman of her wealth. It was uncommon, however, for a woman of her means to allow her daughter to marry outside her status.

"I do say, Charles, the home for my dear Eliza will be most impressive," Mrs. Williams remarked.

"Here Mrs. Williams, won't you allow me to tour you and your daughter around the grounds? In return, I may wish to hear the details of our upcoming nuptials." *A day I most eagerly anticipate*, he thought to himself.

"Oh, what a lovely idea Charles! Eliza was just drafting the invitation list this morning. I do believe her grandmother is coming from London to join in the event."

"Our home is coming along rather nicely Charles. Will it be complete by our day?" Eliza peeped up at his towering frame with her big round eyes, blushing as his own eyes reflected the same adoring look.

Our day. He loved it when she used that phrase. "Yes my dearest, our home is nearly finished now, just a few final touches I'd say. If you look up, you can see Mr. Stuart is completing the chimney, and just inside, the mantels for the parlors are being placed about the hearths in each room. All that's left, I'm pleased to report, are details at this point. And of course, anything you wish the home to boast will immediately be added onto my list."

"Is that certain?" inquired Eliza as the trio glided towards the garden. "Oh then I wish for a gorgeous porch where you and I may rest and watch the twinkling sky in the evening. It should of course round on towards the side of the home, against the dining room, so if you and your gentlemen wish to take a cigar and brandy outdoors, you may do so with ease. As for the garden, surely there will indeed be daisies everywhere? And a swing for afternoon reading?"

"Consider it done my dear." Charles would likely never say no to her.

As they strolled around the three-story home, they

discussed the interior décor style, what color to paint the façade, the new expansive wrap-around porch, and the storage that could be used in the stone basement. Charles showed the ladies where the English garden would be planted in the backyard come the spring season, and lastly, the two stained glass windows he had designed for Eliza. He knew on a sunny day the enchanting sunlight would please her in those front rooms. Charles captivated the ladies with stories of all the balls that Eliza could host so elegantly with the grand stairway in the front foyer. The home would layout nicely for parties.

In return Mrs. Williams regaled the entire wedding ceremony in detail to Charles, most of which he tuned out for another opportunity to study his bride to be. The event would be held just before Christmas, a time Eliza said was magically charming to her. The ceremony itself was to be a traditional Catholic wedding with a dinner and ball to follow at the Williams Manor, located at the top of Forest Hill Road. Charles was too busy being hypnotized by Eliza's gorgeous chocolate eyes to hear the other details though. He truly thought they were the window to her soul, for somebody with the most expressive and beautiful eyes could only be an equally handsome person on the inside in return.

Tingles on his neck caused Charles to suddenly halt mid-step and whip an about-face the opposite direction. Jakob was climbing on a ladder racked against the side of the home, and bouncing on it. The motion was causing the ladder to knock about the pallet of bricks on the roof where the chimney was being shaped.

On instinct, Charles broke into a run towards Jakob when he saw the small boy bounce the ladder again. "Jakob get down! Jakob!" The boy was notorious for getting into messes. The bricks slid further down the pitch of the roof and Charles launched into a sprint, hearing the girls shouting at Jakob from behind. A brick fell, barely missing the child's head. "Jakob get down now!" Charles hurled his body towards the boy and yanked him off the ladder, just as the entire pallet of bricks began to crash off the roof. He tucked and rolled the two of them into the rough trunk of the pine tree on the east side of the home, now covered in red dust from the crash of the freshly demolished bricks.

Eliza reached Charles and Jakob first. "Jakob, are you alright? Charles?" She tugged the boy off of her affianced and into her lap. "You're a magnet for trouble boy. Let me look at you! Are you okay?" She pulled his face towards hers and saw the tears spilling out of her little brother's eyes.

"I hurt Charles! He's bleeding Lizzy!"

Charles held his head up then and Eliza blanched as the bright red liquid trickling out of his hair and down his forehead. It had made her stomach churn with nausea.

"It's just a scrape, Jakob. It isn't even painful. You did, however, challenge my lungs," he wheezed. By the time Mrs. Williams reached the scene, Charles had managed a wink at Eliza to let her know the pain was tolerable.

"Oh Charles you saved him! Jakob you have got to quit scaring me like that. The Lord only knows what happens to you, of course, that your sister *doesn't* let your father and I know about. Let's get you home and in the bath. You are absolutely filthy now." Mrs. Williams graciously thanked Charles again and told Eliza to hurry and she began to push Jakob towards the carriage. "There's a lot to do before the ball this evening and now we have more."

Eliza glanced back at Charles, her eyes sparkling up at him. He was aware she was imaging him trussed up in a coat and tails, as she had been nonchalantly mentioning the ball nearly everyday for the last two weeks. She had told him she was the luckiest girl to have such a handsome man on her arm. Charles always managed to correct her, stating it was the other way around. *He* was the lucky one, of that he was positive.

chapter three.

His eyes were still roaming over her. Sasha had felt
uncomfortable from the moment the man strolled into
the small corner coffee shop. She had been trying to
write about her new Queen Anne Victorian house, just
over on High Street, but hadn't gotten far when the
door chimed and her eyes popped up in time to see him
enter.

Gosh, he was handsome, unparalleled so. Sasha
guessed he was thirty years old or so, and at least six
feet tall. There was a phantom ache in her neck from
the idea of what it would feel like to stare into his eyes.
The blue-gray three piece suit he wore somehow
accentuated his rugged frame, ginger-red hair and
crystal blue eyes. The same eyes that pierced hers when
she first saw him in the doorway - and she had sensed

them on her ever since.

Just keep your head down, act like you're working, Sasha kept telling herself. *Avoid attention.* The pencil in her hand absentmindedly traced doodles in her notebook. *Curious though*, she thought. *He looks Scottish but I didn't see a single freckle on his face. That's odd for a ginger-haired man.* Taking an oversized gulp of her bittersweet mocha, Sasha bent her head down to her lap top once more and started typing.

Why is it so hard to concentrate? I just want to look at him again. He was not exiting her mind as she wished. Was she not used to his unusual eyes? That must be it. She was sure of it. His face was just a novelty.

"Is this seat taken?"

Sasha jumped in her chair, looking up into those pale blue eyes, only this time they were talking to her. She couldn't even speak, too startled from her thoughts. *Was this a small town greeting?* Nobody in the city would ever dare walk up to a stranger. *Apparently, this is country hospitality*, she smirked to herself.

Shaking her head, the pretty blue eyes breezily sat down across from her, and managed to not even so much as blink as it might break their gaze. The owner of the bakeshop smiled as she decorated a wedding cake.

Sasha could feel the woman's giggle as though someone slapped her across the cheek, snapping her back into reality, and broke their staring contest by shutting her laptop.

"You're new here, right? I know everybody in this town."

The hypnotic blue eyes were so warm and generous. *And they come with boyish dimples.*

"My name's Henry." He stuck his hand out and showed off a smile so brilliant it could compete with his eyes. *Almost.*

Somehow she found her vocal cords. "Sasha. I just moved here from New York". Reaching across the table, she shook his hand and instantly became goosepimply all over. Sasha wasn't a believer in love at first site, or even love. But lust…well that was possible.

"Oh right, you bought the house just over on High Street?" The deep timber of his voice sent thrills up her spine.

She was taken aback and arched a curious eyebrow. "Yes that's right, but how did you know that?" Sasha wasn't the biggest fan of receiving attention.

Henry chuckled. "The whole town's talking about it. Don't you know?" He paused for her blush.

"Nobody stays in that house very long. People are placing bets on you." His deep voice had an underlying and velvet-like Southern charm about it. It was soothing.

"Why? They don't even know me. I can handle a small town." Sasha folded her arm, her defensive side up and ready for anything the beautiful strange man could have to say. She didn't like being told the whole town was talking about her. It very much felt like judgment.

Henry's face blanched. He wasn't so attractive then, Sasha almost preferred it. "No! I'm sorry!" his hands offensively flew up, "that came out wrong. It's the *house* the townsfolk are gossiping about." Henry leaned forward. "You see…it's over a hundred years old and said to be haunted by its original mistress. Well, *some* people say that."

Sasha felt her defensive walls drop with ease. "And what do you say, Henry. Is it haunted?"

"No, not in my opinion". He leaned back and took a sip of his tea.

Peppermint? Sasha recognized the smell from her grandmother's trunk, having found an old peppermint oil bottle that had leaked on the interior fabric lining. It was a wonderful reminder of her grandmother and now whenever she opened the lid to the trunk, the minty smell wafted through her senses.

"I think a house can choose its owner sometimes. But you are the one living there. What do you suspect?" he asked, taking another sip of tea.

It was Sasha's turned to grin, "That's how I feel. The house isn't haunted though, you can lay that rumor to rest. I did wonder how some of the original furniture was still there, now I know. It must have been abandoned, everything left behind."

"Have you searched the attic yet? Or the basement? Is it really unfinished?"

"Yes, it's stone. Someone has taken the time to update the plumbing and heating/cooling systems. The ducts are separate though, between stories, so I hope it won't be too expensive to heat." Why was she talking about plumbing and bills? What was wrong with her? *Why do I ramble when I'm nervous!*

There was an awkward silence between them as Sasha idly stirred her coffee without realizing it. Henry appeared to be studying her for an question he already knew the answer to. Sasha nervously chewed on her bottom lip and the silence grew.

"You can read people, can't you Sasha?"

Sasha was taken aback, but nodded her head in

answering, "Yes." She allowed herself to gaze into his eyes then, and she felt her nervousness begin to melt. "Why would you ask that?"

"Because I rather got the impression you were people-watching, just before I entered the shop."

"I was. I like to know people's stories." She let go of her bottom lip.

"Really?" His interest piqued. "What do I do for a living?"

"Lawyer." There was no hesitation in her reply.

"That's amazing. How did you know that?"

A twinkle sparked in her eyes. "You're drinking tea, and there's not nearly as much caffeine in it as in coffee. It'd be awfully bad to be high strung in court. Also, your morning newspaper is turned to the police records, so you're probably wondering who'll be calling you this morning. The suit is pretty snazzy too."

Henry grinned and nodded, "Touché Sasha. Touché."

chapter four.

A week had come and gone since Sasha met Henry, or gone back to the small corner coffee shop. A feeling of hesistancy told her she wasn't ready to encounter him again, or experience the effect his presence seemed to have on her. Still, Sasha could not seem to get those intoxicating blue eyes out of her mind. No work on her novel had begun, she'd barely opened her laptop, and couldn't find inspiration around town to motivate her to even try. She did, however, paint the downstairs bathroom a familiar entransical ice blue.

The connection to the house, on the other hand, seemed stronger than ever. She had told Henry it wasn't haunted, but she was having second thoughts. Often, when she walked through the foyer she felt a presence. It wasn't like she had seen a ghost, but more as though she had once lived in the house before. *And what a crazy thought to entertain.* Even so, she sensed déjà vu. Sasha was able to recognize the oddest things - like a scratch on the floor that came from an old pair of roller skates. It was silly to even let that thought slip into her mind, she knew that, but the sensation was strong. Sasha was from New York; her grandmother was from New York. How could she possibly know the scratch was from a roller skate?

Every house has a story right? I think it's time for this house to tell me why I'm here. Sasha was in the mood to discover, but rather decided it was more like a lesson in history. With her fluffy black cat Hanks in tow, she decided now was the best moment to begin her adventure.

The house was a part of her now, and though the house wasn't scary at all, she still felt nervous as she unlocked the deadbolt to the attic door. The steep narrow stairs were wooden, dusty from abandonment. Flipping the light switch, Sasha took a step, then shivered. There was that old familiar feeling of awareness again, as though she already knew what the attic had to boast.

Sasha told herself that if this was a movie, the background music would sound like an old record player that was tooting the sounds of a violin and piano.

Something intricate, maybe something like Debussy. Yes, that would be very appropriate for the moment.

As she stepped cautiously upwards, letting her cat go first, the idea of spiders trickled into her mind and she gasped, looking upward for cobwebs. The stairs were too sharp vertically, and by not looking at them, she tripped and fell chest forward. Catching herself before there was a chance to have the joy of splinters in her face, she groaned loudly. *Typical Sasha*, she thought, *the girl most likely to walk into walls*. She had a way of attracting accidents and had always been told it ran in the family. Pulling herself up, she rapidly climbed the rest of the stairs, dusting her hands off on her jeans when she reached the top.

Sasha looked around, recognizing her surroundings as though it was a memory from a dream. There were two windows on the south side of the attic, facing away from the river and offered a view of the tree-lined street. The giant wall of the chimney was in the center of the room, thick with aged red brick. Roof nails from each shingle were visible in the low vaulted ceiling. The low lighting gave the attic an intense feeling of familiarity as she walked around the outer edge of the attic first. She stopped to look at some dusty woodwork, and to her surprise, discovered it was the original grand stairway from the foyer, broken into pieces. Though dismantled, someone had kept it with the house. *As it should be.*

Searching onward, a little further along the curve of the wall, she halted once more when she saw a trunk out of the corner of her eye. There, behind an antique dress mannequin, was an emblem she knew well. It was from the 1904 World's Fair, the same as her grandmother's trunk. Moving toward it, she attempted to open the trunk, but discovered it was tightly locked. She jiggled it, hoping the rust would have corroded the metal through. No luck. She looked around at the piled up dusty wood work, mirrors, frames... all furniture.

Where would a key have been kept? Should she get a screwdriver or something to break the lock? No, that seemed wrong somehow. What kind of secrets could be in the trunk? Standing up, she turned and touched the mannequin, and instinctively knew it had once been used for a wedding dress. Sasha shivered with an overwhelming sense of romanticism. Taking in a deep steadying breath, *I'm becoming a sap*, she thought.

Sasha wasn't aware of how long she had been musing over the trunk until the darkness began to settle across the attic. Walking over to the windows to take a peek at the sunset beginning to the night sky, Sasha chuckled to herself as she saw Henry crossing the street towards her house, with a coffee from the corner bakeshop in hand. It was a guess, but it appeared that Henry hadn't been able to stop thinking about her either. As she turned and started back downstairs, she now wondered if those windows hadn't been put in *just* for the purpose of having a look out. Over a hundred years ago, with fewer neighbors, the view would've been great indeed.

Sasha reached her foyer and opened the front door, just as Henry began to knock.

"How'd you do that?" Henry asked, his ready-to-knock fist frozen in the air.

All she saw was blue. "What?" Sasha pushed some of her messy curly hair out of her face in an attempt to collect her thoughts.

"Know I was at the door?"

"I saw you from the window. Is that coffee behind your back for me?"

Looking a bit sheepish for a moment, and not nearly as handsome, Henry swung his left hand around from behind his back, offering the brown and white to-go cup to her. "I hadn't seen you down there lately, and thought you might be going through caffeine withdrawals by now."

Taking the cup, Sasha smiled as she inhaled the scent of a bittersweet mocha, nonfat with no whip. Henry was a man that noticed details. *What a rare specimen of mankind*, she joked to herself.

"So this small town stalker thing you have going on,

does it usually work out for you?"

"Well being a lawyer does come in handy on the stalker bit," he chuckled at Sasha's raised left eyebrow. "But no, I can say that I've honestly never played coffee delivery boy before."

Smiling wide, she opened the door to let him into her foyer. As he breezed passed her, she felt a sudden sense of déjà vu yet again. "You've been in the house before haven't you?" *Blurt things out much Sasha?*

Henry turned with a frown. "How could you have possibly have known that? I barely remember it myself, I was four-years-old."

"You had mentioned knowing the basement was unfinished," Sasha tried to cover her weird-vibes blurt out. "I just assumed," she shrugged. "Let me show you around."

The tour of the downstairs was highlighted by Henry's fascination of the tile work around each fireplace. It was amazing to think of the attention to detail each room maintained over the past century.

As she led him through the kitchen's french doors onto the brick patio, Henry paused.

"No grill?"

Sasha laughed, having heard the question

everywhere she had ever lived. "No, no, I'm a vegetarian. Nothing with a face, that's my motto."

"Oh. And you moved to dairy cow land because..."

"It's a long story." Sasha stared down at the brick patio, rocking back and forth slightly on her heels.

"We can go to this little restaurant around the corner and talk about it," he shoved his hands into his pockets, "if you'd like, I mean. I like long stories."

"Did you just ask me out for a date?" Her right eyebrow arched with an odd mixture of curiosity and suspicion... and excitement?

"I'd prefer if you thought of it has a plate of vegetables."

Sasha laughed. "Well, I could be up for a bit of rabbit food I suppose."

"Did you want to change?"

"Why?" Sasha looked down to notice her dark washed denim jeans covered in dirt and rust. "I was in the attic," she said, as though that explained everything.

As if on cue, her black furball of a cat meowed in the kitchen window, covered whiskers to tail in cobwebs. Hanks was always looking out for her.

chapter five.

This would never happen in the city. Nobody would ever: have, own, operate or even go to a restaurant in a *house*. But yet there she was, walking into a small two-story brick bungalow house with the name of Sloppy Jane's laser cut into the glass of the front door. *Cute name, but an odd location*, in Sasha's opinion. Walking through the entrance, she noticed the first interior room had a small bar on the right and two round tables on the left hand side, just large enough to seat eight people between the two tables. Looking forward, she could see that there were two more dining rooms, each with five more tables. The place was small, but maybe it was adequately appropriate for the size of the town? Sasha's attention was drawn to the female bartender, who was now leaving the space behind the bar, and laying one obviously possessive hand on Henry's arm.

"How many will be joining you tonight Henry?" Her voice was syrupy sweet. Sasha hated it.

"It's just us Alice, table for two."

"So this is what you do on your night off?" Alice responded. "Come to your own restaurant? You're so silly Henry." The woman named Alice glared at Sasha, replacing her flirty smile with a curt nod, so quickly that Henry hadn't seen it. She spun on her heel and led them to a table for four in the room on the left, within view of the bar. Alice dropped the small one-page menus on the table and asked Henry what he would like to drink, delivering one more disapproving look to Sasha before leaving their table. She could've sworn the chick added a bit more of a sway to her hips.

Sasha looked quizzically at Henry. "You own this restaurant?"

"Yes, lawyer by day, bartender by night. Bi-polar careers, I know, I am quite aware of it." There was that fantastic grin again.

"And you named it Sloppy Jane's?"

"Well why should *Joe* get all the credit?"

Sasha laughed, more to herself than for Henry's

benefit. The joke was cheesy but it cracked a smile across her face. It surprised her that Henry would open a restaurant, but then again he did seem to possess a certain charm that probably worked rather well on most of the town. Sasha was becoming very aware of that drool-worthy appeal working on her. Actually, that little factoid was beginning to annoy her. Sasha hadn't picked up her life, literally, and moved halfway across the country to fall under the captivating allure of some small town bachelor. So far, her risk of changing her entire world wasn't lending any inspiration to her writer's block anymore than before. However, as she peeked at the handsome ice blue eyes across from her, Sasha supposed there was no harm in making a friend in the mean time.

After Sasha had to wait to order her drink from the waitress, and the two had ordered their choice of dinner, the discussions were wide open for the twosome. They discussed everything from politics to favorite books - his was To Kill a Mockingbird, hers was Sense & Sensibility - to family, even to Henry's heritage. Sasha had finally looked past his hypnotic azure eyes to notice once again that there were no freckles on this ginger-haired man.

"Yes, I'm really of Scottish decent. But I believe there is some German mixed into that line as well."

"It's just interesting."

39

"And yourself?"

"I've only been told of an English heritage. I was raised by my grandmother from the time I was six, and she only knew of her, well my mother's, side of the family."

"May I ask where your parents were?"

"Car crash. And my father was an orphan prior to being adopted by my grandmother's neighbors, but they passed away before I was born. So… no family tree for my father." Henry appeared saddened by her statement, so Sasha added, "I'm okay with it, really. Don't look so sad. When those things happen so young to a child, it's hard to remember the early memories. I mostly know of only New York and my grandmother."

Sasha leaned forward to blow the small candle out on the table.

"Why'd you do that," asked Henry.

"I am not one for candles, though I should be over it by now."

Henry blinked at Sasha, confused by the phobia.

Awkward. Good job Sasha. "Well, it happened in high school," she began, launching into the story from senior literature class.

"Three weeks into my senior year of high school, I was sitting in my college prep English class, taking a test over Beowulf. The essay exam wasn't hard and I knew it'd only take about ten minutes to complete and this was an hour-long course. Absent-mindedly, I was playing with my hair and looking out the window. You see, the tennis courts were in clear view and I could see the men's weightlifting class doing conditioning exercises, shirtless." *Really, what was a seventeen-year-old girl to do?* Sasha blushed just a bit, but quickly continued, "Getting back to my test, I flipped my hair over my shoulder and began writing the essay. Behind me, I could hear a wrinkling sound, which I mistook for my teacher opening up yet another piece of candy. When I started to get a little hot, I leaned backward in my chair to get some air, and I caught a horrible whiff of a burnt odor." Sasha's eyes mirrored the moment.

"Suddenly, I jumped up with my hands clasping my head, knocking my desk over – which made a horribly loud cluttering sound. My hair had caught fire from a blackberry candle that had been sitting on my teacher's desk. Everybody was staring at me, but nobody helped. I screamed and then my teacher scurried toward me, but I had already managed to pat it out." Idly, Sasha ran her fingertips through her long chocolate hair.

"A few minutes later, after I had calmed down, the teacher brushed a comb through my hair, and this course, thick, burnt chunk of hair broke off from my

41

head. I'm not embarrassed to say I cried. For a teenage girl, that was devastating."

Sasha took a deep breath. "I wore a hat over my head the rest of the day, causing me to receive two after-school detentions. One for wearing the hat which was a dress code violation, and another for refusing to remove it." She smiled at that little rebellion. "Needless to say, I got an A on my test."

Henry laughed but caught the look on Sasha's face and turned it into a cough. "You should tell that anecdote at parties." He paused as she stirred her drink. "Well, I won't let this candle on the table light your hair up. I promise, Scout's Honor." Taking a lighter out of his pocket, Henry re-lit the little white candle, and then winked at Sasha. "I think it's time to fight your fears."

Sasha shyly laughed back and nodded. There was little awkward lull in the conversation as she stared at the flickering flame. *It's such a silly fear, really.*

"Why did you move here?" Henry jump-started the conversation.

"To solve a mystery."

"A mystery?" Henry looked doubtful. "In this town?"

Sasha took a sip of the cocktail she had been

unconsciously stirring. "Yes. My grandmother left me an old trunk after she passed away, and inside was a photograph." She paused for dramatic effect, stirring her cocktail once more, "a photograph of the house over on High Street." Sasha decided to omit the details of the matching trunk in the attic with the 1904 World's Fair emblem on it. "It intrigued me to the point of no return. This house has a story, I am sure of it. So here I am."

Looking puzzled, Henry sat his drink down, and stared only a second or three at it before he leaned forward, clasping his hands under his chin. "And what have you found?"

"A lock."

"Lock?"

"Yes and it needs a key."

"Can't you just break it?"

"Oh no. It's an antique lock. Plus, what if I'm not meant to see what's inside?" Sasha, mimicking his move, leaned forward, piquing Henry's interest just a little more. "But if I find the key, then I'll know I was meant to open it."

Leaning back into her chair once more, Sasha tasted another sip of her cocktail, since it was now mixed quite well. "Tell me something. Why'd you open a restaurant with a girl's name?"

Thrown by the topic, Henry wasn't quite as smooth with his answer. Sasha realized she preferred it when he stuttered. *It's like making a Greek God a mortal. A very attractive mortal.* She may not be interested in a relationship for the time being, but she wasn't daft enough to deny how attractive the man was.

"I… uh… well the idea just popped into my head one day. I'd wanted to open a pub for a very long time, but I just didn't want to be stereotypical with the whole 'I'm Scottish' bit. I've enjoyed every minute of owning the restaurant, and it's been open for three years now."

"It's very nice."

chapter six.

Charles couldn't believe his own eyesight. Every opportunity he gained to see his breathtaking fiancé, he swore she was more beautiful than the time before. There she was, right next to the baker and his wife, spinning like a vision of gold thread about the dance floor. Charles was sure he was not the only soul enthralled by Eliza, as the whole town - including the Judge – seemed to have their eyes magnetically glued to the dancing beauty. Honestly, it was no wonder, really, that every person in attendance had fallen under Eliza's spell. Who wouldn't? Her gleaming dark espresso mane was cascading down her back - curl after curl - sparkled like a gemstone. The cut of her gold hued gown was stitched with an ivory lace overlay that made her thin body even more curvaceous than he personally thought was necessary - what, with so many men in attendance – and her porcelain skin was practically glowing with the laughter on her lips. Her constant enjoyment of the evening left a faint trace of light pink across her high cheekbones and a twinkle of delight in her eyes. She was every bit the Belle of the ball, no doubt about that. *And she's going to marry me, a lowly pub owner*, Charles thought.

The house on High Street was being built to satisfy her father. Eliza had told him repeatedly she didn't care if they lived in a broom closet, as long as they were incandescently in love and blissfully married. Charles loved her all the more for the fact that Eliza didn't care about societal formalities. The Judge wanted her to stay high in the ranks of wealth and class, and it wasn't that Charles was un-wealthy; he just wasn't rich in her father's eyes. As it was, liquor wealth was not considered old family money, but the Judge respected that it was hard earned money.

So Charles designed the house with Eliza's details, and assisted in the construction of the architecture, splitting his time between the pub and the development. His good friend Andrew was the helping to manage the pub when Charles couldn't be there. With the exterior nearly finished, Charles thought the rooms would be fully furnished by the time of their wedding. Eliza was sure to love every area of the dwelling, as she selected all the furnishings.

Snapping out of his musings, Charles shook his head with laughter as he saw Mrs. Williams scolding Jakob, who had now spilled chocolate pudding down his junior tux and her skirt. He wasn't sure he had ever been around the boy when he hadn't attracted some sort of accident. He and Eliza had even placed bets before on what could happen and when. She typically found herself on the winner's side as it was intuition for her. 'It's a *feeling* I have,' she would state, and she was usually right. As his eyes drifted back to her, he thought about how it was quirky, in the best way, and only added to her charming existence. *Really, too bad women aren't allowed to gamble.*

"She's absolutely amazing. Are you sure I'm not supposed to be the one marrying her?"

His thoughts now interrupted once more, Charles rolled his eyes at his good mate Andrew. "I find it difficult to believe I let you talk me into closing Scottie's down for an evening just so you could attend the ball and stare at *my* fiancé."

"I'm still finding it difficult to believe she chose you, when she could've chosen *me*." Andrew mocked his charismatically good looks, showing the truth of his ever-teasing nature, by batting his eyelashes over his emerald eyes at Charles.

In truth, Andrew was typically the more handsome

47

of the two ever-so striking gentlemen. He was the tall, dark and handsome variety, the Mayor's son, and packaged with a rakish smile combined with a devil-may-care attitude. Though Charles was tall, he was much leaner in muscle, had the palest ice blue eyes anybody has ever seen, ginger hair that glowed with a bronze tint in the sunlight and not a single freckle on his tanned Scottish body. Charles acknowledged his looks were more unique in interest.

"You'll just have to settle for Annabelle mate," Charles acquiesced, referring to Andrew's own affianced. "It's not like you don't have an angel of your own."

A roguish grin immediately plastered across Andrew's face with the picture Annabelle Cooper in his mind. Annabelle was the town physician's daughter and Eliza's dearest friend. She was on the floor engaged in a dance of her own with her older and much more serious-toned brother Edward. As greatly as she loved and desired amusement in her daily life, he wanted a no-nonsense nature in his own. Her father was elderly and Edward had taken it upon himself to be a very protective sibling. He had given Andrew - a vastly skilled pugilist – an honest run for his money once or twice in several rounds of fisticuffs, and that was after Andrew obtained permission for Annabelle's hand in marriage, though it was to be a long engagement.

"Annabelle is quite something," Andrew smirked at Charles. Annabelle was smiling towards the two of them with a dazzling expression. Her honey blonde hair swept high off her neck in a mess of ringlets and Annabelle's big sapphire eyes sparkled against her silver and ocean blue gown. Though her hair was fair, her skin had much more of a tan than Sasha's, meaning her cheeks didn't show blushes quite as well. This was something Charles surely wouldn't like. The beautiful friend of Eliza's had never known her mother, as she had died in child birth, and Charles was positive the reason Edward was so protective of her was that Annabelle must strongly resemble the late Mrs. Cooper. He was also certain that it was the same reasoning that Mr. Cooper never attended the balls as Annabelle's escort, as it must be too painful for him, too much of a memory.

"I believe this dance is yours, Sir."

Looking into his fiancés smiling eyes, Charles met them with his own eager anticipation. "I believe your dance card is mine for the rest of our lives." Looping her arms through his, Charles led her back the way in which she had weaved herself through the dance floor mere moments earlier, stopping close to the open floor length glass doors. "You know, our wedding ball will be the crème de la crème of the county in just a few months time. Then I will be dancing with my wife," he smiled as he gazed adoringly into her chocolate eyes.

Sighing with blissful contentment as she fit into his arms like a glove, they stepped exquisitely into a waltz. Charles never pulled his gaze from her eyes. She was so content to just be with him. Every time they danced or would stroll through the local park, she just appeared to be in a heavenly dream. Twirling her intentionally towards the open doorway, Charles took their waltz onto the balcony like it was part of a brilliantly choreographed routine. The two continued to twirl to the far side of the terrace, to the place where any window no longer invaded their privacy, and his supportive arms now wrapped more tightly around her waist. Drawing her close, he leaned his upper body down so she could wrap her dainty hands around his neck, helping her pull herself up on her tip toes.

"You're a devilish rake, Charles."

"Oh you love me though, my darling. Would you ever have me any other way?"

Eliza paused to think about it, as if she seriously needed time to ponder the question, and smirking as she giggled the words "of course not!"

It was during these moments - when they kissed under the twinkling light of the stars, under their own veil of privacy, with music setting the mood in the background and shivers of electricity running through their veins – in which Charles wished they could just cross two county lines and elope.

chapter seven.

The same continuously guilt-ridden dream had been haunting Sasha for the past six months. Every time, she awoke gasping, "I'm sorry!" Frantically looking around her bedroom, she recognized she wasn't in New York anymore. Hanks was curled up at the foot of her bed snoring softly, completely undisturbed by her night terror outburst.

The guilt was over the death of her grandmother. While she had been dying in her bed for months, Sasha had been there for her every step of the way. On her grandmother's last night, she had convinced Sasha to go out with her friends for an evening, that what she needed was for Sasha to be young and to live while she could. Sasha went and when she got the call at the club, she had never felt more ashamed of herself. Her grandmother had passed away while she was laughing and having a good time. It was a selfish act.

Grief overwhelmed Sasha. She had practically been on the floor in tears she was sobbing so hard at the funeral service. It had been the only time she cried, really cried. The absence of her parental figure had left a gaping hole in her chest. Had her grandmother known that it would be her last evening? Had she? Would she have not wanted her granddaughter, who was more like a daughter, around for her last moment or two of life? Had she thought it would too painful for Sasha?

When this same dream and emotional process woke her up again on this significantly cooler September morning, Sasha decided 4:30am was not too early to start her day. She flung her legs off her antique, white wrought-iron bed and felt around with her toes for her slippers. Finding them slightly pushed under her bed, Sasha grabbed her glasses off the nightstand, trudging her way to the stairs, and flopped her slippers down all nineteen steps. While Sasha was used to her elevator for her city apartment, she had found herself counting the stairs every time she went up or down the stairwell. It wasn't long before she realized she had developed this little OCD habit, but yet she didn't mind it. Chalking it up to extra detail, she thought it was necessary to learn the house inside and out if she ever hoped to write about it.

Grabbing her coffee out of the freezer, a sleep-deprived Sasha found this humorous enough to manage a smile so early in the morning. The corner bakeshop owner had told her the freezer acts as a preservative and kept the grounds fresh, giving a better taste. Sasha hadn't the slightest clue if that was true or not, but she decided to pick up that habit as well. As she brewed a giant pot for herself, Sasha saw those blue eyes in her mind again and scowled.

She could not let herself think about him. Never had she let a man control her life and Sasha prided herself in being totally independent. She had never had the desire of children or marriage. It just wasn't something she desired or felt as though she *had* to do. It was stereotypical for people to assume otherwise. She wasn't the little girl who grew up dreaming of white gowns and fairytales. It just wasn't Sasha.

Henry had even asked her on a date after diner at Sloppy Jane's the other night, after they went on an evening stroll around downtown. She had told him she wasn't interested in dating at the moment, but really liked being friends with him. She knew it sounded like a cheesy line, but it was true to her very core. She *wasn't* interested in dating. Dating led to relationships, and serious discussions, and nobody ever understood her issues with marriage and children. *And well, all things permanent*, she admitted to herself. Sasha couldn't even bring herself to get a tattoo because it was too much of a commitment. The only man in her life was her cat, and Hanks was a shadow to her every move at home.

The disappointment had shown on Henry's face, but he seemed to understand, and still invited her to his restaurant this Saturday. Apparently there was a 'Backyard Bash' or something to that effect. Whatever it was, it sounded truly small town and Sasha had told him she wasn't sure. Now that she found herself picturing those crystal-clear turquoise eyes, she definitely wasn't sure.

While she was aware her stubbornness was her most adamant character flaw, she also knew there was her terrified fear of being hurt. Just because she may not believe in love, that didn't mean she couldn't be hurt. She had her walls up and her trust was not earned easily, if at all. She liked Henry, and she was very attracted to him, but she could control herself. *I can, darn it.*

The full pot of vanilla flavored coffee was nearly empty before she realized she had been curled up in a blanket, staring into the backyard for nearly three hours. The sun was up and some of the mist from the river had drifted into her almost garden. She sighed as she thought of the beauty it could truly be by spring.

Within the hour Sasha had managed to pull herself

out of her funk and decided to walk around town. Grabbing her camera and a notebook, she stepped out her front door, turning away from the direction of downtown. She decided to move east, walking up High Street to look at the other homes, some older than hers. Not really having wondered around the neighborhood much yet, she started to fall for the lure of the quaint town all over again.

Diagonally across from her house was an off-white two-story Colonial style home that had originally been a log cabin. The plaque on the sidewalk explained that the home first belonged to the founding father of the town. Up the street just two houses further was a rose colored Victorian larger than her own new abode, though it had no stain glass windows in the front windows on display. Sasha knew no other way of describing the house other than by writing down 'pink girly dream home' in her notebook. Between this house and the next was a gravel lot overlooking the river, and then yet another Queen Anne Victorian, even more ornate than the last. There was a huge wrap-a-round porch that reminded Sasha of the South. She imagined ladies stitching bonnets and reading the latest great American novel. It was a chocolate and pale yellow, and was so large that the family must've been very wealthy. She could envision a man in a dark three-piece suit and a pocket watch sitting on a rocking chair and sipping a mint julep.

Smiling to herself, she continued her leisurely walk. The next house was different than the others. It was Italianate and located on the bluffs overlooking the Missouri River. It was older, maybe circa 1840. Just by looking at it, she knew this house had twelve-foot ceilings and had ten-foot windows, elaborate plaster moldings and interior shutters. It was simply gorgeous and obviously constructed for a prominent family. Sasha imagined the house to be gorgeous at Christmas time.

Sasha turned right from there and circled back to the downtown area, which was really only one long street, Main Street. Avoiding passing by Henry's law office, she ambled about five blocks further when she discovered herself standing in front of an old theatre - Boone's Opera Hall. There was something magical about the historical playhouse, and she was tickled by a new place to explore and the endless possibilities of those who had been there before her. Her high-heeled boots tapped on the stone steps as she climbed them. Taking a breath, Sasha reached out and tried the door. It was open. As she timidly stepped inside, she inhaled a big whiff, smelling the old chairs, the Hollywood-style red curtains, the orchestra pit and the slight musk from being closed up.

The front office was vacated, so she granted herself permission to continue wondering through the front of the house. Just before reaching the aisle of four hundred chairs, a plaque on the wall caught her attention, bringing her to a halt. It was a history of the building.

Boone's Opera Hall was the oldest theater west of the Alleghenies, *wherever those are*, she thought. And it was still in use by the local arts in town. Originally an opera house, the classically beautiful red brick theatre first opened with a grand ball on July 3, 1857. *A grand ball? How magical*, she thought. The ball was held just short of two years after laying the cornerstone of the foundation. For more than seventy years, history recycled the use of Boone's Opera Hall and its community. The theatre had survived the Civil War, having been used for a hospital during those years, and was once an actual movie theatre in the 1960's. At one point, the structure even hosted a skating rink in the basement. Presently, the theatre was restored to its glory and currently used as a playhouse venue for the town.

Sasha was impressed that a community could find so many ways to utilize a building. As she turned and walked through the entryway into the aisles, she was delighted to see the red plush velvet seats, the old glamour of the stage curtains with delicate gold trim, original box seats that were so beautifully crafted and ornate with matching gold trim, and the mezzanine balcony for higher viewing. Looking towards the ceiling, she was thrilled to see the spotlight machines. Did they highlight a tiny ballerina twirling about the apron cover once upon a time? Sasha hummed a bit of Chopin to herself as she continued her solo tour of her majestic discovery.

As she moved to climb on top of the apron covering the orchestra pit, she imagined high society ladies in the box seats and wondered what that must have felt like. Was it every bit as grand as she dreamt of? Her hands touched the red velvet of the curtains, searching for the split in the fabric and Sasha ducked her way through to the stage. The lights were on but she still saw nobody around. She deeply inhaled once more. The smell was musky, in a good sort of way. On the back wall she could see names carved into the brick of past performers, allowing for the slightest hint of romanticism of a ghost. Yes, Boone's Opera Hall had retained a classic elegance for a piece of history more than one hundred and fifty years old. It was almost indescribable. The rustic smell of the old furniture, the trim of the aged show business curtains, the original box seats, the whispers of the wind blowing when the stage-door was left open, and the mutter of the aching stage floors as she moved across them. Sasha could definitely find a way to incorporate the edifice of what seemed like merely a distant memory into her book. Closing her eyes, Sasha felt the ghost of theatre's past dance around her, welcoming her presence.

Wanting to take a peek at the dressing rooms, she moved toward the stage wings, freezing when she

60

heard the sound of metal scraping above her. Her eyes snapped up to the rafters just in time to see a blue stage light break off its hinges! Trying to back away too fast, she tripped over her own feet, yelping as she fell backwards, her head making a dull thudding sound as it hit the black wooden floor. Vaguely, Sasha heard a man curse above her, followed by the sound of his boots scurrying down a ladder behind the wings.

A deep country accent washed over her senses in a flurry of words. "Are you alright? I am so sorry! I've been replacing those gels all morning and that one must've been rusty too." A hand fluttered over her face. "Ma'am? You in there?" The male voice sounded rushed and alarmed.

Sasha felt a strong arm under her aching head, and another checking her pulse on her wrist. His rough calloused fingers quite warm against her cooler skin. She groaned so he would know the patient was alive - albeit extremely heavy lidded for the time being.

"Oh thank God. I am so sorry." The deeply timbered voice was noticeably relieved.

Using all the effort she could muster, Sasha peeked to try and see who kept apologizing to her with a voice thickly drenched in a country accent, deep and mesmerizing. *Was she dreaming?* When her eyes focused, she saw round emerald eyes focusing anxiously on her with concern. As she opened her eyes wider she saw him relax a bit, probably only just realizing she was going to survive. Any attempt to sit up quickly failed on Sasha, as she became overtaken with dizziness.

"Oh too soon, too soon to move," she muttered for herself, rather than the green-eyed stranger. *Don't throw up, don't throw up, do NOT throw up,* her thoughts chanted.

"Just relax ma'am. Take some deep breaths. I'm *real* sorry."

"Ma'am is somebody much older than me. And quit saying you are sorry. I tripped over my own feet. Help me sit up *please*." Bossiness was part of her honed defense mechanism skills from years in the city. The moment she snapped at the stranger, Sasha could practically hear him roll his eyes at her as she felt his strong hand wrap around her shoulders, braced her, and slowly lifted her into a sitting position. His arm remained wrapped around her for support.

"Better Ma'---Miss?"

Sasha could see his face more clearly now and noticed that along with green bejeweled orbs, the handsome stranger had a few slight freckles dusted across the bridge of his nose and a dimple on decorating right side of his mouth. He had a rugged sense about him with his chestnut hair appearing a little like a shaggy bed head look, a two-day-old shave of whiskers appearing scruffy along his jaw. Mr. Tall, Dark and Handsome himself had just picked her up off a dirty floor as though she were no heavier than a crumpled piece of parchment paper.

Realizing she was staring - possibly drooling - Sasha coughed to break the spell. Glancing to her left, she saw the stage light was now shattered in a million tiny pieces.

"Was that expensive?"

Mr. Tall, Dark and Handsome chuckled, "Maybe. But it would've been replaced anyhow."

Blinking back at him, she realized he still didn't know her name. "I'm Sasha. I'm sorry if I'm intruding, nobody was up front. I just wanted to look around." *How dumb can I sound?*

Something registered in his eyes at her for a moment, before he replied, "I'm Luke. What do you think of the place? I mean, besides the bad handyman?" He locked his arm that was still around her shoulders and hauled her the rest of the way up to a standing position, but didn't let go right away, making sure she was sturdy on her feet.

"This theatre is breathtaking, there's so much history here. And don't worry about the light, it was not

63

your fault. I have been known to attract strange accidents."

They chuckled together and she learned he had volunteered to help in fixing the place up as a favor. Luke's family had donated a lot of money and free labor to the historical board in order to keep the playhouse in working condition. By trade, he was actually an agricultural man.

The twosome had stood there for a while talking about the history of the theatre, until Sasha's roaring stomach reminded her that she'd been up most of the day, hadn't eaten yet, and it was now nearly noon. Her 4:30am wake up call had not held her appetite back.

"I think we should feed you, it'll help you feel better. Let me clean up the glass from the gel light, and I'll take you to this place just down the street. You'll love it." Quickly, Luke dashed off for a broom before she could kindly refuse, and Sasha Reeds was pretty sure she had just made another new friend.

- - -

The walk to the pub grub eatery was halfway from to Sasha's home from Boone's Opera Hall. Luke, having been from a well-established family in the area and knowing more than his share of stories, filled her in on more of the sensationalized nonsense revolving around her new home.

Apparently the place had been abandoned after a horrible accident involving the mistress's younger brother, who was said to have been a magnet for disasters. Sasha had snorted at that bit of commentary, as she definitely had something in common with the boy. Luke had told her the story of how the boy died, but was a little fuzzy with the details. Some townsfolk say he drowned in the river, others said it had been a fire in the old shoe factory.

"There are so many rumors and stories that have been spread over the years, that no one knows what the truth is. Well, except for the fact that it was abandoned, and no new owner has stayed very long. I think most folk just naturally assume it's haunted."

Sasha could understand that, she supposed. Although she had felt a presence, she wasn't sure it was a ghost. Something was tugging at the corner of her thoughts, the place in her mind she couldn't quite see. Giving up on what was bothering her, she glanced around the restaurant.

Sage's Bar & Grill was a hole-in-the-wall place on Main Street. It was absolutely tiny and totally amazing in Sasha's eyes. It couldn't have been more than ten feet wide but it was maybe thirty feet long until a wall, which was hiding the kitchen, cut off the room. Behind the lengthy bar was a matching elongated mirror that displayed the entire room and everybody in it. The walls were teal, the ceiling was tin, and the front bay windows allowed diners to watch life pass by like a television show. Luke was right - she did love it.

Impressing Sasha even further was the fact that there were vegetarian options on the menu, including a garden burger. But she found herself gagging a bit over how many fried things were also on the menu: green beans, cheese, pickles, zucchini, onions, jalapeños and ... *a Twinkie*?

"What exactly is a fried Twinkie?"

When Luke laughed it was a sound so deep and hearty, Sasha could not even attempt to resist a smile. She already knew when he was laughing at her or with her. This time she was sure it was at her, but she didn't really mind. *In this town, it probably is a silly question.*

"A deep fried Twinkie is about the most dangerous creation a restaurant could possibly ever come up with because they are amazing. Truly, I don't even care for sweets or even Twinkies in general, but alas this has not stopped me from liking this gooey, melt-in-your-mouth dessert. I don't even care that it's bad for me. We'll have to order one for you, Yank."

He had a deep humorous gleam in his eye like it was outrageous that Sasha wouldn't know what could be so delicious about fried foods. She was from New York City, she had heard of unhealthy and delectable food. She just preferred hers to be served by a street vendor going by the name of Big Papa.

"Well…. we'll see about that. I don't think it would go so well with a garden burger."

"Vegetarian?"

For some unknown reason, Sasha blushed. *Was she insulting a man who was obviously a farmer*? "Yes."

Luke leaned back in his chair, locking his hands behind his chestnut head and studied her face. "You shouldn't blush so much. It's distracting."

"What?" she said quizzically. Her hands instinctively flew to her face as she blushed again to her ears. Sure enough, they were flaming hot.

"It makes you even more pretty."

And somehow, maybe it was because of the thick country accent, his statement sounded honest and sincere. Sasha was flattered. "What are you doing Saturday night," she asked. "Want to go to that backyard party thing? I keep hearing about it."

Before he could answer, the waitress showed up with his sweet tea and her diet soda. Nodding quickly in answer, he proceeded to order two deep fried Twinkies.

"You know, you shouldn't flatter women so much.

As it is, you aren't exactly hurting my eyesight." *Not one bit*, Sasha thought. But no matter how bright his emerald eyes shined, it was nothing compared to the intoxicating blue color she had become fascinated with.

"I should probably mention I'm engaged," Luke announced, looking a little embarrassed at receiving his own compliment. "Yes, yes… I'm definitely supposed to mention that."

Laughter flowed from Sasha with an effervescent jubilant glee. "Guess we'll just have to be friends then!"

chapter eight.

Sasha couldn't decide how she felt, exactly, about this evening. She was excited to hang out with Luke again, and to meet his fiancée, but was nervous about those familiar ice blue eyes. It was as though she had electrocuting butterflies in her stomach. Looking in her full-length mirror to see if the feeling transcended to her appearance, she frowned. *Just my eyes.* Overall, Sasha thought she pretty good, actually, having tried real hard not to dress too club-like, too New York, too… *city*. While she doubted her clothing attire would keep the attention off of the girl who bought the allegedly haunting High Street house, it was worth a shot.

Sasha hated attention and often felt like she stood out too much in this town. The brand new glistening white Lexus RC with taupe leather interior in the driveway probably didn't help. In the city, she wouldn't have thought of it, because back home everybody in her daily life had money and fancy things. Compared to her friend's vehicles, Sasha was slumming it. Here in this small town, less seemed to always be more. It was an idea she was quickly conditioning herself to, and liking the changes.

Turning in the mirror to study her outfit one more time, she felt satisfied with her reflection. It was a cooler evening, so she had chosen a pair of dark, stretchy skinny jeans to wear with simple knee high black boots with a low heel, a simple black skinny belt and a black three-quartered sleeve shirt with an asymmetrical cut neck. Black was really her signature color - it's what she was always the most comfortable in. In fact, most of her closet was full of black apparel and high heels and designer handbags.

Biting her bottom lip, Sasha studied her face now, playing with the small silver cross around her neck. She had done a tiny bit of a smoky eye using taupe and violet eye shadows, because she knew it only enhanced her chocolate eyes. Having left her long dark hair loose and curly for the evening, and with a tiny bit of color on her cheeks and whisper pink lips, Sasha thought she looked kind of pretty.

And at the same instance, Sasha couldn't figure out why she cared. She didn't know these people and it's not as if she could possibly remember every person she'd encounter tonight. Hanks meowed at her from the bed, and she swore he had this 'Don't play dumb' look on his furry face. *Ugh…. there were those electrocuting butterflies again*. Sasha groaned inwardly, just in time to hear the doorbell.

The wide smile plastered across her features quickly dropped off the face of the planet when Sasha opened the door to see Luke standing with Alice, holding hands. That was his fiancée! Rude and disdainful Alice! Her excitement all but plopped into the taste of mud in her mouth, while the butterflies closed their wings and went back into their cocoons.

Luke's handsome smile was not going to right this ship. "Sasha, this is Alice. She's been dying to meet you."

What? Alice had not mentioned anything about the first meeting? Or had Alice not known who she was that night at the restaurant? *Oh of course she knows who I am! The whole darn town has done nothing but whisper about the girl who purchased the house on High Street.*

Alice stood there with only a smile on her face, showing no hint of their prior meeting. Sasha stepped back and let the happy couple enter into her foyer.

"Hello Alice, I'm Sasha. It's nice to meet you." Alice

71

hugged her. She *hugged* her. *Is this girl bipolar or something?*

"Hi Sasha. Your house is amazing!" Alice was eyeing Sasha's baby grand piano in the parlor.

Yep, definitely bipolar. Sasha glanced behind herself at Luke and he appeared, like most men, oblivious of the small tension she was exuding. In fact, he was only really watching Alice, and Sasha realized that he was totally smitten. For him, she'd give Alice a second chance. Luke was too good of a man to not have exemplary taste in the woman he'd chosen to marry. Taking a deep breath, she turned back to Alice, whose eyes were glazed over after spying a small decoration on the mantle above the parlor fireplace. It was the jeweled box Sasha had found in the attic just that morning, though she did not think the jewels were real and she had found it empty inside.

Sasha studied Alice for a moment. The first time she had seen her, Alice had her chin-length blonde hair in curls, but now she was wearing it with more of a pixie cut, a spiky bob and just a little messy. It was pretty cute, actually. And the girl was about Sasha's height of five foot six, though just a bit more slender in her frame, and her round blue-bejeweled eyes twinkled as she took in her new surroundings. Sasha could swear she had a smile she was trying to hide. Alice and Luke did look as though they would fit well together. Yes, she would give Alice another chance.

"Do you like it Alice?"

Realizing then that Sasha and Luke had been being watched her, the glaze in her eyes disappeared. "Mmmm," she said. "It is very unique. Did you bring it from New York?"

Sasha stepped towards the box and reached to pull it down from the mantel. "No, actually, I didn't. I found it here, in the attic just this morning. You see I've been searching through the stuff up there, just a little at a time. This house is simply full of treasures." She placed the box in Alice's hands, "but I'm finding there's so much to get distracted by."

Alice studied the box and Sasha swore that the little blue sapphires adorning the trinket sparkled more brilliantly more in her hands. "Was there anything in it?"

"No not at all. I found it in a hat box with nothing else."

Alice placed it back on the mantle and smiled at Sasha. "It's wonderful. I wonder what else is up there."

Sasha had to agree.

It was then that Luke decided it was time to get the show on the road. Sasha grabbed her lemon-yellow clutch, the only color in her outfit, and within two minutes they were halfway to Sloppy Jane's. Alice kept up the conversation now and it was as if their first meeting had never happened. Luke seemed annoyed with the amount of girly chatter and giggles, but Sasha had to presume he was exaggerating a tiny bit. The walk was less than five minutes in total, but the information Alice had filled in her on could've been its own book. The wealth of information she'd been given just now was astounding. Sasha idly wondered if there was a town gossip blog she could follow, as it may be easier to keep up with.

As it happened, Alice and Luke were good friends of Henry's. *Does it seem like the whole town is connected to him*, her mind wondered. In school they had been amply titled as the Three Amigo's. Alice only worked an evening or two a week to help Henry out when he was short staffed or Luke was going to be working in the fields late. Sasha was surprised to learn Alice had a day job as the town pharmacist. She said Henry only wanted people behind the bar that he could trust when he, himself wasn't going to there. Sasha thought that made sense, and now that she knew Henry trusted Alice too, she was sure Alice had probably just been protective of her friend that evening.

Apparently Henry was the small town's resident bachelor as well, never having a girlfriend longer than a month. Alice informed her that he would always chalk it up to there being no chemistry, or that he wasn't interested in dating anybody, and that he was a workaholic by nature.

"It's not that women don't try - *many* try," Alice explained. "But Henry always says when he finds the right person, that it would feel as though time stood still."

When Sasha heard that statement, she wasn't sure if she should question the man's sanity or not. *A man being a hopeless romantic?* That was a first for her. There weren't too many of those, if any, in the city, so to hear this about Henry left her feeling a bit gobsmacked. She wasn't sure she was ready to process the information.

The entrance to the backyard party wasn't through the restaurant, as Sasha assumed it would be, but around the side of the bungalow-styled brick house. There was a tall wooden fence encasing the backyard, providing privacy to those who entered. The woman collecting entry fees at the door let all three of them through the gate without paying, winking at Luke. *But who wouldn't, really*. Sasha was amazed – the place was packed. There were so many people she had to wonder where they all came from! She had, in no way, seen this many patrons in one place in this small town. The feeling of such a surprise turnout left her overwhelmed.

The shock didn't keep her from noticing the goose bumps covering her arms as she became aware of the people already staring at her. She allowed her vision to un-focus a bit, blurring the faces of those who were so keen to invade her consciousness. *Are they wondering who the intruder is? Or just deciding which rumors are true?* Alice sensed Sasha's uncomfortable awkwardness and laced an arm through hers, leading them to the main bar. When her eyes refocused, she found herself seeing blue.

- - -

Sasha wasn't sure exactly how many hours had passed or even how many sweet and sour mixes she had drank, but she was acutely aware of the fact she was now wearing glow-in-the-dark necklaces around her neck and wrists. Plus, she'd witnessed Henry feeling triumphant over his win of a one-lap tricycle race against twenty other guys in wranglers and cowboy boots.

Alice had quickly apologized for acting like a complete and formidable jerk when they'd first met, which Sasha graciously accepted. Luke had persuaded her to dance to a song from a famous eighty's movie soundtrack, which left Sasha feeling inadequate from her dance moves and short of breath from laughing. *And...* she knew she was having a really awesome time. Alice told her it was small town magic. The voice in

Sasha's mind told her it was two too many drinks, and Henry told her it was because she wanted to let loose of the city. Sasha realized that it was entirely possible for all those things to be true. Contentment filled her in that moment, as she was sincerely grateful for her new friends.

Unsure she could dance anymore or laugh any harder, alarmed distress punched her in the gut when she suddenly felt herself being roughly pulled from the picnic table she had been perched on top of just seconds earlier, reflecting on her good fortune.

Sasha was not happy to discover it wasn't Luke or Henry's arms she was held in, but a rather fat, balding, middle-aged man who looked three sheets to the wind. As he slurred whiskey-written words into her ear, most of which she could barely hear against the music, panic began to choke her as bells of anxiety began to agitate her mind. Her skin crawled as she felt his roaming hands move over her body and Sasha tried to pull herself free from his pudgy fingers.

"Look here strange girl, you can dance with me. It's ok to meet new peeeopleee," the mustached man garbled as his he stumbled, which placed more of his weight on her as the drunk stepped hard on her left foot.

"Ow! Get off me!" As the pain registered, she

snapped out of the frozen fright bubble that had trapped her seconds earlier, and was once more attempting to escape out of his greasy web, when she felt a pair of strong arms yank her safely away - into a rock solid chest. A sense of ease and security blanketed her instantly. However, the tone of the usually good natured jolly voice she heard jolted her back to her alarmed state, too quickly for her satisfaction. She wanted to crawl right back into her new security blanket.

"Get out of here John. There's already a cab waiting and paid for."

"Aw listen Henry, we were just making acquaintances, becomin' friendsss..." he teetered back.

"John, you are on probation and aren't supposed to drink for two years. You're lucky it's not the cops I have waiting for you. Out!"

He stepped close enough now that Sasha could smell the whiskey on his breath. "Seeee ya later sweetheart."

As his watery eyes roamed over her body, Sasha involuntarily shivered. In less than a second later, she felt Henry's arm tighten around her waist even firmer, and she relaxed again.

Henry nodded to Luke in the doorway and Sasha

watched as he disappeared, stepping out of the fenced area to ensure John got in the cab. Twirling Sasha around to face him, relief washed over Henry's face, and she saw blue once more. The azure hue was different this time – filled with concern, anger and something else Sasha was unable to name.

"I'm okay Henry, really. Totally fine." Swallowing any remaining anxiety that could still be in her throat, she pulled herself out of his arms, stepping away from his reach as her face flushed with the realization that no one else in the backyard seemed to have even noticed the altercation that just occurred. An altercation, that to her, had felt like a hugely aggressive and invasive attack to her personal space.

Abruptly, she realized just how out of her trust bubble she was and how vulnerable that had left her. Looking back at the ice blues eyes that had brought her instant relief, she could see how tense Henry had become…and still was. He appeared as though his Scottish temper was winning a battle.

Suddenly, Sasha wanted nothing more to be at her house; curled up in bed with her black cat, Hanks, and to leave this night behind her. She wanted her walls back up, for people to stop their incessant chatter about the girl who was living in the High Street house… she wanted to be alone.

"I'm going to leave Henry. This just became a little too much for me. Thank you, it was fun. Until, well you know," her face flushed again. "Tell Alice and Luke thanks as well." Giving him a quick, friendly hug, she dashed towards the gate while he was still too tense to move. She'd buy him a tea at the corner coffee shop Monday morning to thank him or something. Maybe a doughnut too. Yes a doughnut with cream and jelly or maybe even a scone? Sasha's thoughts were scattered beyond even her comprehension. *Why am I so rattled?* Ducking around the corner on the house, and on to the sidewalk, she smacked right into Luke.

"Oh!" She felt his hands grab her shoulders to steady her. Sasha was grateful for not falling on her butt.

"Sasha! Whoa, where's the fire?" His friendly eyes were filled with worry.

"It's late. I just want to go home. I'm tired." She forced a yawn for his benefit. "Tell Alice I'll call her tomorrow."

Luke, always the gentleman, offered to walk her home, but Sasha didn't want the company. No, she only wanted to be alone. It was something she was good at. Thanking him, but showing him her pepper spray she had placed inside her lemon yellow clutch, Sasha told him she had a really good high kick that could take off anybody's head.

Letting out a laugh, Luke let her walk home by herself. But Sasha knew he'd stood there, on the sidewalk outside of Sloppy Jane's, long enough to watch her walk straight to High Street. She'd sensed his eyes on her back the entire walk home, until she took a right and strolled out of his view. She liked her new friend.

chapter nine.

"Where did you run off to Saturday night? One minute, we're dancing, then, I go to the bathroom and when I return, Poof! You are gone. I missed the drunken John scene entirely." Alice stirred her to-go coffee from the corner coffee shop as the two women sat on the front porch, breaking in Sasha's new white wicker furniture.

At some point during the backyard party, Alice had offered to search and organize the attic Monday morning. Sasha completely forgot about it, too, until Alice knocked on her door that morning, complete with beverages and bagels in hand.

"Well the drunken John scene involved me. I was too uncomfortable to hang around after that."

Alice's eyes widened. "Luke didn't tell me it was you he was groping. You should know that John is the biggest lush in the tri-county area. And if he had been sober," she paused, "well, honestly, you would've been raked over the coals. He finds something wrong with everybody. The man is lewd and cruel. And I imagine lonely because of it, or because of his loneliness he's horrid? Hard to say which came first really. "

Sasha shook her head. "I'm irritated with myself really. I can handle incorrigible men like that – I would've handled John!" She felt her defensive walls creep up like a shield around her. "I was just thrown off when Henry was suddenly there, pulling me out of the situation. It threw me off balance. I couldn't think straight." She looked up to the clouds and inhaled the deep smell of the rain that hadn't yet begun to pour. The scent smoothed her frazzled nerves.

A small twinkle popped into Alice's eyes, leaving her looking mischievous in every way. "You like Henry," she said in such a simplistic manner that it left no illusion of the statement ever being a question.

"As a friend."

"Sasha, you like him. Admit it."

"It doesn't matter Alice. I don't believe in love. And I'm not about to break hearts I can't fix."

84

Alice's twinkle faded. "Who says you'll break his heart?"

"It's what I do." Sasha shrugged her slouched shoulders again the white wicker chair, her whole face remaining blank and completely void of emotion. It was a comfortable place for her to dwell in. "I run away from all things permanent and serious and anything that screams commitment. *Nothing* is forever."

"Have you always been like this?"

"Pretty much."

"Can I ask why?"

Sasha looked at Alice. Her friend looked heartbroken over that fact the Sasha basically couldn't feel *anything*. She had been numb forever. The only exception was her grandmother's funeral. She had been the only person Sasha had ever kept in her heart. "My parents died when I was six. The only family I had was my grandmother. I guess I've always just accepted that it was my fate to be alone." In truth, Sasha learned all too early what the hollow loss of losing those she cared about felt like. Having never wanted to let her grandmother know, Sasha hid the fact she remembered the pain of that particular heartbreak, and she wasn't keen to find it again.

Alice shook her head. "Or maybe you were meant

to be here, to find your family? Friends can be that, you know, family. Maybe your grandmother knew something you didn't? Why else would she have known about this house?"

Sasha stood brushing her jeans off with her hands as it she was dusting off the topic of conversation. "I don't know. Grab your coffee and we can go find out. Besides, it's about to rain." *Why did grandmother set her on this wild chase?* The question had crossed her mind several times.

Alice was about to object to Sasha's weather report when, sure enough, the clouds opened and started to pour, and the two girls ran inside.

- - -

Hours were spent in the attic that day. The girls had opened the two south facing windows, which had allowed the smell of rain fill the room in its entirety. The room had an eerie effect that day with the hanging light bulbs providing shadowed light across the attic. Sasha still had not found the key to the 1904 World's Fair trunk from St. Louis. She, however, did find many other clunky, leather-beaten worn trunks though, and those were unlocked. Lining every truck into a queue to be carried down the steep stairs so they could open them in better light. Alice had made a valid point that antique luggage should hold a lot of surprises. The rain was enchanting their mood of adventure and discovery, the smell becoming intoxicating. It was the same smell, no matter where it poured in the world. Rain was always the same; consistent and comforting.

Inside an old hat box, Alice came across old photograph and correspondence in the form of letters and cards. The ink was rather worn and the papers crinkled, but the photos were still in good condition. Alice studied the images, one by one, until she something that caused her to gasp sharply, dropping the hatbox and spilling its contents all over the dusty attic floor.

"Sasha! It's you!"

Sasha rolled her eyes. *So dramatic,* she thought, moving closer to see the photo. "Don't be so theatrical Alice. Obviously it can't be me."

Alice's eyes were still huge as saucers as she handed the photo over and Sasha stepped closer to the one on of the few light bulbs in the attic. Her mouth dropped open as her eyes focused on the woman holding center court in the photo. *Okay, so there's some resemblance.* Actually there was quite a lot of resemblance. *It's uncanny.*

In her hand was a photo of what appeared to be a family. The woman who mostly resembled Sasha was in the middle of the large group, holding a small child in her hands and another child, a toddler, was hugging her right leg. To her left was a handsome, tall and lean gentleman decked out in a suit with eyes so light they barely showed up in the photo at all. On his side, a more muscular man with dark hair and an arm wrapped around a lady who looked like an old fashioned version of Alice, with her long curly fair hair that was tied with a ribbon. They, too, had a child that was standing with his small body wrapped completely around his father's riding boots. On the other side was an older couple, who appeared as though they were holding a secret. Sasha's stomach plummeted as she realized the older lady looked too much like her grandmother that it began to unsettle her stomach. The only face she didn't recognize whatsoever was that of a younger male standing with the older couple. He was a young man that looked very similar in appearance to Sasha, with dark curly hair and big round eyes. He must be her look-a-like's brother. *This is weird, so weird.*

"Alice, you have ties to this town, right?"

Alice had finally picked up her own slacked jaw and walked to where Sasha was standing, frozen in confusion of the photo's aftermath. "I do. My great grandfather was the town's physician, only physician actually. I was always told that I inherit my love of medicine from him."

"Oh. Okay. Did you not happen to notice that you

88

are in this photo too? See?" Sasha waved the picture in her face, "and look whom you are standing next to."

"What?" She grabbed the photo back and gasped yet again. "Luke!"

"I know. Did you see who's by me?"

"Henry. Well that's no surprise really. It's fate."

"No surprise? Gag me, Alice, please. Fate? Really?"

"Oh I'm sorry! Are you going to explain this hundred-year-old photo as something else? And did you happen to see what is in our hands?" Alice jabbed her finger at the photo as if it weren't obvious where to look already.

Sasha again grabbed the photo from Alice's clutching fingers. There, in her lap with the little girl, was a small, jeweled box that matched the one she had found in the attic, the same one that had bewitched Alice two nights ago. Each woman in the photo had one. The two kids standing were holding ice cream cones. *This background looks like… fair grounds!*

"Alice! This photo!"

"I know!"

"No, I mean, yes!" Sasha became quickly animated, recognizing a clue that Alice had inadvertently discovered. "But it was taken at the world's fair! It was at the 1904 fair where the ice cream cone was invented and introduced! And we know the original owners of this house were there because of the mysterious locked trunk over in the corner! My grandmother had a matching trunk that I brought with me. It's where I found the photo of this house." When she'd first come across the picture of the High Street house, instinct told her the photograph was meant for her to find. Now, she felt her intuition was confirmed.

Alice shivered, "creepy."

Sasha couldn't agree more. Flipping the photo over, she read a small caption in the most scribbled handwriting 'Charles and Eliza Hoffmeister - 1904'.

chapter ten.

Charles wasn't aware of the seemingly thousands of candles creating the fiery glow surrounding him. Nor was he aware that every inch of surface appeared to be covered in white roses and green garland, creating a sweet smell through the holiday air. He did not feel the cool breeze from the snowflakes falling from the clouds or even sense the hundred pairs of eyes on him. No, all Charles could see was Eliza. Eliza Hoffmeister. His wife. He smiled broadly at the actuality of the word *wife*. From the moment he'd peered into her chocolate eyes, she hadn't left his thoughts. In was in those next moments following that comprehension when he realized he never wanted her to.

The couple wed only a week before Christmas. Her parents had kept the affair moderately simple. Only a hundred or so were on the invitation list, which was relatively small for the Judge's only daughter joining another in Holy Matrimony. And it was a perfect union in Charles's eyes.

He thought the music for their wedding waltz was ideal as well, as they gracefully danced the swirling motions throughout the luminous ballroom. Eliza had chosen Claude Debussy's *Claire de Lune* to be performed for them by a young pianist. She had once told Charles that she'd fallen in love with the story behind the piece. Named for Paul Verlaine's poem "Clair de Lune", the title of the song was also French for the word 'moonlight', which was sentimental to the newly wedded pair as they often gazed at the stars in the evening, leaving only the man in the moon to keep the couple company.

Eliza was always elegant and charming, but on this evening her chocolate eyes were sparkling with a dazzling glimmer from the antique gold gown she was wearing, and the glow of all the soft illumination around the couple gave her the shine of an angel. Happiness was radiating from every ounce of the pair. During the vows, his own eyes had glossed over as he slid a delicate diamond and gold band, with a gold vine wrapped around the symbol of his commitment, on her ring finger.

The couple was only made aware that the waltz

had ended when Andrew and Annabelle joined the pair on the ballroom floor, followed closely by other guests. The twosome had been utterly enveloped into a starry-eyed gaze with one another, dancing in their own world. Charles watched Eliza give a small delicate wave with her lace-gloved hand, smiling at the baker and his wife. Eliza wasn't spoiled or vain with any of her relationships in life nor did she fall in line with high society rules. She chose her friends 'in accordance to the heart', she always said.

In accordance to the heart. Charles knew precisely what she meant. Eliza was pulled to life in the same manner in which he was pulled towards her. The heart knew everything, and it was always correct. *In accordance to the heart*. Charles had believed in the phrase so much he had inquired to the Priest to include it in their ceremony and vows. The strong phrase was also engraved on the interior of Eliza's wedding band. It would be a fine surprise to excite her with once they were alone.

Charles's trail of thoughts broke has he felt an annoying tap on his shoulder, hearing Eliza's giggle as he rolled in eyes towards the ceiling in a silent prayer.

"Can I dance with the bride? I solemnly swear to take impeccable care of her for you."

Charles felt as though he could punch Andrew,

which of course the ballsy charmer was probably expecting. Giving a serious expression to Eliza, "if he even so much as steps on a toe, tell me. Nothing harms my *wife*." Charles smiled a wide grin at the word *wife* again. The man just wasn't able to help it, his ice blue eyes shined brightly with the word.

"Charles, darling, you've been waiting to say *wife* all night, haven't you?" Eliza's smile was breathtaking. "Not that I mind, of course." She delightfully winked and stepped out of her new husband's embrace and into Andrew's.

"Take care of Annabelle, mate. I'm watching you too." Andrew chuckled, always the playful one of the fateful foursome of friends. He whirled Eliza about ten paces a way, just out of hearing range.

"Andrew, must you tease him?" Eliza chided, "You, of all people, should know how protective of his loved ones Charles can be." Eliza's smile seemed to become larger - if possible - at the idea of how much Charles cared about those in his life. It was a dazzling grin that could break any man.

"Oh I trust in that, Liz. I wouldn't leave Annabelle with just anybody on the dance floor," he said with a twinkling sense of humor, but not enough that anybody could mistake the seriousness of the statement. That was a gift of Andrew's, his ability of mixing such charismatic sweetness with such utter sincerity. "I've never seen him so serene. Do you know the effect you have on him Liz? As long as he knows where you are, and that you're are happy in life, he's practically harmonious in the head."

"Harmonious in the head?"

"That statement almost certainly did not reflect my sentiment in the manner I would've preferred it to sound. What I mean is that Charles is content. He is so at ease now. I never thought he would find love. It could have been Annabelle and I forever, with Charles as our forever third. He could have been our child, in a manner of speaking."

Eliza hadn't really heard the end of the statement. "How could somebody not fall in love with Charles?"

"I didn't say women didn't want him. Hells bells, there's an entire clan of unhappy wives who cannot help themselves but to bat their eyelashes at the man. He is absolutely, ignorantly oblivious towards those women and their wasted attempts." Andrew brought his emerald eyes level to her own sparkling brown eyes, "he told me with you that it was instantaneous. His heart said yes the minute he saw you sprinting, *quite* unabashedly I hear, through his pub after Jakob. He was impressed by the lengths you would go to protect your young and impressionable brother."

"That young and impressionable brother of mine is a risk beggar for life. I have to watch him closely." Jakob was six years old and it had become the extended family joke that if Jakob was around, and something wasn't broken yet, it probably would be in due time.

Andrew started to speak once more, when he was cut off by the crashing sound behind his back. Every person in the ballroom spun out of their waltz to see Jakob climbing off the floor, brushing off his junior tuxedo, which was now covered in champagne and strawberries.

Eliza laughed, shaking her head.

"What's so funny?" Andrew appeared as though he was embarrassed on behalf of young Jakob, and Eliza's pretty head shook even more from her laughter.

"I just won another wager against Charles!" The glee was not held back in her tone. "He thought for sure it would be a carriage incident that went awry, but I said 'No, it will be somewhere with glass'. Oh Jakob."

Both Andrew and Eliza laughed now as they turned towards Charles, who knew he just lost the bet. He let his head and shoulders droop in defeat. Her instincts were always on the button and Charles always lost his wagers with Eliza.

chapter eleven.

Nearly two months had passed by since Alice found that photo of what Sasha now saw as her previous life. She wasn't exactly sure how or why it had become so easy to accept that, but she had so often felt moments of déjà vu in this town, that it made sense. But that day in the attic started to freak her out, so Sasha slowed her visits upstairs down to once a week, until the dreams began. Items and stories started to visit Sasha in her unconsciousness and showed her what to find and where things were hidden. Even creepier was that fact that all the dreams were *almost* always true. There was only one exception. Repeatedly she often dreamt that when she tried to open the locked trunk, that was a sister to her grandmother's piece, that she had the key already safely stowed in her pocket. But Sasha didn't have the key or even know where to look for it. It ticked her off that her subconscious mind was telling her she had the answer when she clearly couldn't figure it out.

The next time she had seen Henry had been awkward. Neither person brought up John, or the fact Sasha had freaked out at the party. But still...they had the awkward pausing and the swimming around for something to talk about moment, and Sasha just kept seeing the old faded photograph in her mind with Alice saying, "It's fate". She couldn't think straight on a normal day around Henry and now she was just glad he couldn't read her mind.

It wasn't until about a week later that conversation seemed normal between them again. In fact, she felt a little bit like Henry was courting her friendship, always showing up wherever she was, with the always ever-charming thing to say. That is, until the morning Sasha walked into the corner bakeshop and was immediately tackled by a little boy with blonde hair and bright blue eyes. The kid was maybe seven-years-old and was sick – that was obvious to Sasha.

"What's your name?" Sasha knelt down in front of him smiling, please when he smiled back.

The boy definitely wasn't shy. "Evan Michael. Most people call me Ev. What's your name? You sure are pretty Ma'am. You should marry my Uncle. He's always been single."

Sasha chuckled at his enthusiasm. The boy may have been sickly, but he was full of spirit. "My name is Sasha."

"And yes she is pretty Evan, but she would never admit it," a familiar voice had said.

As Sasha glanced up at Henry, her smiling face turning shy, and her stomach fluttering as he returned the expression. Sasha could practically hear the grin on the shop owner's face.

"Do you know her, Uncle Henry?" The boy was still attached to Sasha's leg, though rather weakly.

"Oh he's knows me," Sasha had stated with more sarcasm than Henry could understand, which was confirmed by the peculiar look briefly crossing his handsome features.

"Will you join us for a hot apple cider ma'am?" the little boy asked. "They pour lots of yummy caramel and whip cream on it!"

"Well! How could I resist that?" Sasha laughed.

- - -

That chance meeting of Evan inspired Sasha to host a charity event in her home on Halloween, an All

Hallows' Eve Masquerade Ball. Working together with Alice, the two sold tickets from the pharmacy, bakeshop and at Sloppy Jane's, and gathered up twenty women, ages twenty one to forty five to be humorously auctioned off for a good cause. All the money raised was going to support the nearby children's hospital, a place specifically for children with leukemia - kids like Evan. Though she didn't have the luxury of having the boy in her life for very long, Evan had woven a thread around Sasha's heart like a lasso so strongly that he'd felt like a nephew of her own.

Alice chose Halloween for the event having said it was her favorite holiday. Sasha didn't really agree with her about that, as she was more of a Christmas season fan, but she did rather like the sound of a ball. The High Street house was the perfect setting, *and* she already had the perfect dress.

Hidden away inside one of the trunks Alice and she had discovered was the most gorgeous gown either of them had ever seen - and just her size. Alice starting drooling about fate again, but Sasha ignored her and studied the dress. The hand stitched gold material was very fancy with an elegant ivory lace overlay and champagne trim, which would shine with her pale skin and dark hair. The bodice of the gown had a corset fit and would probably be uncomfortable, but the beauty of the gown would be worth the pain. It was a dress for a princess.

100

After they had found the dress, the decorations were designed to revolve around it for the theme. Champagne with strawberries was being served upon entry, and twinkle lights were covering every flowerbed and tree, as well as the porch spindles and walkways. Ivory candles were in the windows with a clear-glassed cylinder cover encasing the flames. All of the tablecloths were ivory with champagne lace with gold stitching. Every piece of material used was a lighter shade of gold and every flower was pearl white, with the exception of the arrangement gracing the black baby grand piano, which was a large bouquet of dark, blood red roses. It was simply dreamy. *It was magical*, Sasha thought.

Sasha and Alice prepared for the charity ball together, and included Evan's mom and Henry's sister, Olivia. Sasha was sure the event would be too difficult for her since Evan had passed a month ago, but Olivia swore that her little Evan Michael would want her to fight for the children who still had time. Sasha deeply admired Olivia for her strength. In fact, they had turned out to be close friends, but not as close as her and Alice. After the night of the backyard party, their bond was inconceivably tight, as though they'd known each other all their lives.

However, like Alice - and the entire town it seemed - Olivia wanted to know why she wasn't dating Henry yet. The two women would go on and on for hours about how he longed for her. *Pure exaggeration*, Sasha told herself every time. *Henry is a good friend, that's all. Okay, so he's fun and good looking, and yeah... we sometimes flirt. Friends can flirt.* In truth, he was now a part of Sasha's daily life too.

"Group photo!" Alice screamed. "After all, we are dashing in our finery!"

Sasha was in her gold dress with her naturally curly espresso hair tied back with a piece of lace. Olivia was wearing an emerald colored prom gown that had been trimmed with black lace and a sheer black overlay to make it look a bit more like an old fashioned in style. Alice had found another dress in one of the attic trunks, and though it was a day dress, it was still exquisite on her. It was a light aqua-blue silk empire waist ensemble with a square neck. She purchased a pair of ivory silk gloves from a thrift shop, and wore her grandmother's pearls to dress it up. With her hair in curls, pinned loosely into a bun, Alice was stunning. In fact, all three women were stunning.

It seemed like ages had gone by before the camera timer set off, and the women ended up laughing so hard, their photo became a silly, goofy, intentionally candid moment. Alice swore the ladies could not retake the picture because, "the best pictures are those that are caught in the moment."

Sasha left the ladies to go downstairs, barefoot, to

light all the candles. She was midway through the foyer when her feet froze in their tracks, as she realized not only were all the candles lit and flaming, all the twinkle lights were plugged in. Her home was glowing! Every corner was shimmering in radiant light.

Then, there was the music. It was Henry, slightly hidden behind the bloodstained roses, and playing something familiar. *Beethoven?* Sasha stood frozen in awe inside the pocket doorway between the foyer and parlor. *I had no idea he played. And so beautifully!* Just when she felt like she knew him – and was comfortable with that idea – he turned another facet out. Gooseflesh covered her arms, alerting her sense to how much she admired Henry playing the piano with his bartending, law-abiding hands. The electrocuting butterflies were back in her stomach forcing her to acknowledge how handsome he was in a tuxedo. Her heart was impressed that he didn't even seem to know she was standing there with her mouth gaping open and watching him. She was afraid to move, not wanting him to stop playing, as Sasha was busy eating the sight up with her eyes.

Finally, she took a step forward and his eyes lifted up meet her gaze. A particular shade of crystal blue was quickly becoming her favorite color. She moved over to sit on the piano bench next to him. Henry only smiled back and began playing a Debussy piece, one that made her think of moonlight. Sasha was impressed, really impressed.

- - -

The enchanted evening went as smoothly as Sasha could've prayed for and the event had raised nearly ten thousand dollars in Evan Michael's memory. Sasha intended to match that donation with money from the trust fund her grandmother had left her.

Once the auction was complete, the night continued on with lively music and dancing. The guests surprised her with their talents while performing karaoke on the piano as well. Sasha was impressed with the show of talent this small town possessed, but wasn't about to sing herself. Alice did manage to convince Sasha to play the baby grand piano for a while as she sang a popular country song by some girl who clearly liked a good love story. Sasha had never heard it before but found she liked Alice's rendition. Luke, who just seemed more charming by the moment, had brought his Gibson and sang an original tune.

It surprised Sasha at how comfortable she was feeling with her new friends. She had felt oddly in a haze the whole night with an overwhelming sense of Déjà Vu again. Maybe it was the photo in the attic with her face on it or the gold dress she was wearing. She didn't really know but it was almost as if she was living a memory from a dream.

104

Just as she was walking back in to the kitchen for more strawberries she bumped into Henry and thought for a moment that the 'bumping into' had been on purpose. Then she knew it indeed had been on purpose when she saw the twitches of a smile in the corners of his mouth.

"I was just about to get some air. Would you like to go with me?" Henry held his elbow up for her to loop her arm through.

Sasha smiled at Grace, the owner of the corner coffee shop as they passed her, toasting her husband cheerfully, and felt her cheeks pink up a bit as she saw the lady wink at her, like she knew all along that the two would hit it off. *Was the whole world conspiring?*

Sasha linked her arm through Henry's and let him escort outside to the brick patio, smiling as she took in the ferociously twinkling lights glowing in the darkness, the night sky beautifully covered by a partly cloudy but still moonlit sky. Unintentionally, she shivered from the perfection of being alone with a man whom she had feelings for. *I may as well admit to myself what the whole town can see.* Sasha was going to stop fighting what seemed inevitable, letting go of her comfort zone and its numbing sensation. She refused to call it fate though. It was maybe a coincidence, but not fate. But she did feel deeply for Henry and the awareness of that thought made her want to turn around and run. The touch of his warm fingers on her arm, however, cindered her nervousness, replacing it with excitement… and even some anxiousness she admitted to herself.

Henry, mistaking her shiver for coldness, took off his tuxedo jacket and laid it carefully on her shoulders. She didn't discourage him, not when the jacket smelled of peppermint, such a familiar and soothing smell. She didn't remember the party or the guests anymore. Sasha felt as though she and Henry were completely alone in a very picturesque, romantic setting. There were no secrets, no deep fears. No longer was she consumed with worry about her heart being broken. The moment felt so accurate, so true - true to her exact heart's accordance. The phrase was so accurate. Anymore, Sasha was to the point of only feeling alive when she was with him. It was Henry who had brought her back to life in this small, tiny little town after her grandmother passed away. Somehow, he managed his way through the maze of her walls, patiently allowing her to make the choice for herself, to realize her own heart. *Why had she tried so hard to deny her feelings?*

"What are you thinking about?" Henry gave her the time to let her thoughts wander about, but his curiosity was trying his patience.

"Henry, doesn't it feel like we've been here before?" Nodding his head in understanding, Sasha

106

knew Henry was aware of what she meant by the question.

Looking up to the midnight sky, he let out a deep sigh. "That's exactly how it feels." Grabbing her hand, Henry yanked her down on to one of the benches she'd placed in her garden. "I don't want this to sound cheesy, but I fear there isn't really any hope for it. I'm completely and incandescently smitten and intrigued by you Sasha." He rushed on before she could cut him off. "It's not just that you look absolutely amazing in that dress - but by the way - you do. I think it's the way that I always know when you enter a room, even if my back is turned. Or maybe it's how you try so hard to not let people get to know you, but yet I do. I know you loved your grandmother more than your own life. I know you're scared of somebody touching your heart because you feel like it's been broken all of your life."

"I never told you th--!"

He cut her off again. "You never had to. It's like I just know you, Sasha. I know you are right handed, but eat dinner with your left hand. You stir your drink with a straw when in deep thought. I know you love rainstorms, especially when thunder and lighting are involved. You have a laugh that is contagious, yet you save it for genuine occasions. I know that you run your hands through your hair when you are frustrated, and that alone makes me want you. I'm absent-minded when you aren't nearby."

Sasha blushed.

"And when you blush like that, it drives me crazy insane." He stood up; throwing his hands to his own head, then took a breath for a moment. "I also know that you hate attention. I admire that even though you do, you threw a benefit in my nephew's memory. I know you would protect your friends at any cost to your own pride. I know I'm connected to you, Sasha, and I would never do a thing to change it. It's as though I've known you my whole life and maybe even before. Sasha, you are the other half of my heart. This... I just know."

Sasha just stared at him. Normally she would have laughed at something like this. But now she didn't know what to do. Part of her wanted grab him and pull him into a kiss. The other part wanted to cry. Did he know about the photo? Had he know they were together in another lifetime? Would he have fallen for somebody else if she had never moved here? She couldn't think clearly anymore, her thoughts were scattered and she had to swallow her rising anxiety. The tears were winning and her natural instincts told her to run away.

As if it was on cue, it somehow started to rain and she let the tears fall. She didn't give up on the other part of herself though and stood up, too short to meet

Henry's face with her own, even with heels. Sasha wrapped her arms around his neck and pulled his head down until his lips met her salty tear stained mouth. It was a kiss that sent her electrocuting butterflies all over her body. A kiss that made her toes curl and her cheeks turn a deep crimson tone. He wrapped his strong arms around her, pulling her into his own frame as though they were puzzle pieces with a perfect fit.

It could have been days before they parted, both oblivious to the rain and anything else. It suddenly clicked in Sasha's head that she had to tell him about the photo. It was only fair to let him know that there had never been any hope, that they were re-born souls just waiting to meet each other in a new life, or fate, coincidence or *something*.

She placed a hand on his chest and pushed herself a way, her tears all dried up in the pounding rain. "Tomorrow, there's something you have to see. It's in the attic."

chapter twelve.

"How's your book coming along?"

The small corner coffee shop had become a daily fix for Sasha. It was no major chain store, it had no Wi-Fi, but yet, it was satisfying in a cozy and comforting manner. She was oddly at home here. In fact, the whole town was really starting to mess with her senses like that. The owner, whose named Sasha has discovered was Grace Hatfield, always asked the right questions at the most appropriate times. It was just so easy to converse with Grace. She was a born nurturer who always knew what others needed.

And though Sasha's book was coming along, it was inching at a snail's pace. So, she figured the perfect cure for writers block was to talk about the characters and Grace had become her essential person to discuss it with. She never spoke about it with Henry or Alice. With Henry, she thought she'd feel too embarrassed. With Alice, bless her heart, Sasha was afraid wouldn't want to *stop* talking about the book. But Grace had this uncanny ability to know when it was always the correct moment in time to drop a subject.

Sasha set her peppermint mocha, the holiday special drink, down on the table, sloshing it a bit, and gave Grace a small apologetic grimace for her lack of grace. "I feel like Drake should offer to stay in the small town to win Sophie's heart. He shouldn't write the article that could tear her family apart. But is that too cliché?"

"Well does he genuinely love Sophie? Or is he just using her emotions for the goods?"

Sasha couldn't answer the question; she didn't know what genuine love was. She herself felt she could live without Henry. She just wasn't going to and had told herself they were two very different things. She was making the conscious choice to stay in Henry's world. She and Alice had even let Henry and Luke in on the old faded photograph and Alice's fate concept. Like men, the two just accepted it and moved on with life. *Such simplistic creatures*, Sasha mused.

Grace took the pause as a time to go take her cake out of the oven and Sasha stared out the window into the snow. Snow was white and pristine, peaceful but yet destructive really. She really wanted to go play in it, make snow angels and sip hot cocoa.

Her Lexus hadn't done so well in the cold weather and she had decided to get a Chevy truck after she had gotten her car stuck on the railroad tracks looking at the frozen river. Luckily no train was coming, but unfortunately the three more months of winter were inevitable. With Henry on her every move and a pickup to drive about town, she had no trouble fitting in at all anymore. She still refused to participate in karaoke with Alice, having been asked multiple times, but she *had* taken up line dancing. Sasha grimaced at the thought of other people's toes having paid the piper a few times.

As she saw a figure move past the window, Sasha closed her laptop just has Henry slipped into the door with the sound of bells. Snow had kissed his ice blue stocking cap, dark grey pea coat and black snow boots.

Showing off those dimples of his that could almost compete with his immaculate eyes, he grinned as he said, "Another angel's got its wings." Henry glanced upwards towards the bells.

Sasha nodded in agreement as he bent down to properly greet her with a kiss. "Do you want to play in the snow?" Sasha blushed as she asked, feeling a bit childish.

Henry cupped her cheek and let his finger trace her blush. "I'm already ahead of you. Luke has sleds out at his farm, a pond for skating and we're picking up Alice from the pharmacy on our way there." The scent of the coffee Sasha was sipping on caught his attention. "Peppermint?"

She blushed a bit more fiercely at his knowing look. When they came to the small corner coffee shop together, she ordered a mocha and he ordered peppermint tea. But when she came alone, she combined the flavors because he always tasted of peppermint when they kissed and she felt it kept Henry close to her when he wasn't around. It was another silly quirk of hers that she had recently picked up. She would've never been this into a guy in New York. No, the once closely guarded person Sasha once was would have kept her head down and never engaged in the banter the two exchanged when they'd first met.

"Yes, it's a peppermint mocha. It's practically like drinking Christmas in a cup."

He laughed, always going along with her quirks. The man was perfect in that way. Sometimes it scared Sasha though, how much he knew her. Just before the first snow of the season he had bought her a big warm and fluffy coat, black of course. But what had amazed her more was the color of the interior, which was ice blue, the color of his pale mesmerizing eyes. She had never told him how much she had been attracted to him in the beginning just because of his gorgeous eyes but yet, he knew.

Henry constantly mentioned her eyes though. She had to finally tell him she didn't like compliments very much, they always made her feel very awkward. He told her she should never feel awkward around him. She did though. And he never pushed her with her feelings either, never asked her to talk about things before she was ready. Still, she had too many walls up and he wasn't about to throw a sledgehammer at her.

"Are you ready to go?"

"Sure, but can we take my truck? I kind of like driving it." She grabbed her laptop and notes and threw them into her tartan plaid designer bag she refused to give up just because she was now the proud owner of a pickup truck in mid-Missouri.

"Wow before long I'll be seeing you in cowboy boots. But slow it down this time with your lead foot, eh? You make me fear for my life sometimes." There was that goofy grin.

She swatted him and waved to Grace, who was sampling the frosting for the red velvet cake that she

115

had just iced, perfect as usual.

Stepping outside was like somebody had punched Sasha in the face with an ice cube. *Or a whole bucket full*, she thought. It was the coldest winter the small town had experienced in the last two decades. In fact, the word 'cold' couldn't really begin to describe the gooseflesh the frigid temperatures gave her. Somehow it was a different type of cold than in New York. She unlocked her glossy black truck and slid in just as quickly as Henry had, starting it up and turning the heat on high.

"If you're that cold already, maybe we shouldn't play in the snow?"

"Bite your tongue, lawyer."

Once they picked Alice up from her pharmacy it was none stop chatter about Christmas and New Year's Eve. She had been planning a party out at Luke's, but wasn't sure how the weather would hold up. Sasha let her know she had a feeling the weather would be fine and Alice took her word for it, as if it were a solid enough reason to believe daisies could bloom on ice.

- - -

"I'm still saying the snowball to the head was a little unnecessary," Alice pouted. She was curled on the sofa with her feet in Luke's lap, but giving Henry an evil eye that was one for the record book.

Sasha couldn't help but laugh once Henry began chuckling, his deep timbre of a voice was so intoxicating. Warmly she was curled up next to him on another plush sofa adjacent to spot where Alice was still glaring. Every time she felt Henry's rib cage ripple, she giggled and Alice mustered up even more irritation in her pretty face.

"Babe, let it go" Luke was laughing too; it was a deep, hearty kind of laugh that was so boyish and fun. "You hit me in the face with two handfuls of snow. Am I complaining?"

"You.Are.A.Boy," Alice bit out, but she fought a smile as she said it, a clear sign she was over it.

They all let their giggles die out as they listened to the fire crackling inside Luke's house. His basement was refinished to feel more like a cabin. Sasha had made them all Hot-Buttered Rum to warm them up and Alice had brought the ingredients for both a vegetarian and regular chili, which they could smell cooking from the kitchen.

There was only about thirty seconds of silence when Alice couldn't take it anymore. "Sasha, you should write about Charles and Eliza!" She was so enthusiastic it threw Sasha off a bit.

"What?" *Where did that suddenly come from?*

"For your book, you should write about Charles and Eliza." Alice paused for a moment, before continuing, "and us."

Sasha took a deep breath. Alice had not been able to drop the idea that the four of them were reincarnated souls, meant to be with each other. The problem Sasha had with this is that she did not know how the story of Charles and Eliza ended.

"Alice, don't you think we're seeing ourselves in that photo because maybe we want too? Maybe it's the New Yorker in me, but how is that possible? I have my grandmother's trunk, so wouldn't she be the reincarnated one? And, quite frankly, I'm not wild about the idea that everything I've gone through in life was fated to be because I'm a reincarnated soul." *I want to believe my choices in life were of my own freewill.* She looked at Alice who was facing Luke now, but she was sure Alice was rolling her eyes. "Besides, out of all the letters and journals I've read, I feel like I knew Andrew and Charles pretty well and I doubt they would chuck snowballs at their women."

Henry looked at Luke, grabbed his heart and mockingly stated, "ouch."

"She's right, Henry!" Alice's evil glare was back.

"Alice, if you hadn't gotten in the way I would've hit Luke!"

"You were aiming for me this whole time? Henry," Luke mocked, "the nerve!"

chapter thirteen.

Sasha sighed in contentment as she woke up in her own bed on New Year's Day, facing Henry. As she pushed herself up on her elbows, she noticed two things right away. First, both of them were still fully clothed from last night, right down to the party hats they had worn at Alice's insistence. Second, Hanks had nestled his way in between them the way a child would, as if to separate them. Smiling, she ran her hand across the sleeping belly of the black furball, letting him purr in response.

Reaching up to pull off the holiday light-up tiara from her head, Sasha placed it on the pillow where she had been laying just moments before. Swinging her legs off the bed as carefully as possible, she left the bedroom, pulling the door softly shut behind her. Pausing, she heard Henry snore softly in his sleep, undisturbed by her movements.

Trudging down the stairs in her sleepy state to the kitchen, Sasha grinned as she watched the snow shower outside. As she predicted to Alice weeks before, the weather had indeed held up until this morning, making the New Years Eve party perfect. Sasha thought about how much she felt like she was part of a snow globe when she watched the weather from inside her antique home. Retrieving the bag of caramel donut flavored coffee from of her freezer, she poured a strong helping of grounds into her coffee maker.

After turning the machine on, Sasha sat down at her table, opened her laptop and began to write. Words flowed easily from her brain to her fingertips, the keys clicking away on the keyboard. Finding a way to drop her barriers – her ever-strong emotional walls - with Henry brought forth an abundance of stories through her mind in a steady stream. Concepts were swimming around her mind and she had begun to write a fictional love story that wasn't about her house at all. One day, she would tell the story or Charles and Eliza, but she needed to know how it ended first. No, instead she decided to write about a first time romance, having been inspired by her own life these days.

When the pot of caramel coffee was half gone, and

the snow continued to increase to blizzard-like standards, Sasha saved her work and shut her laptop. Filling her oversized holiday mug with one more cup of coffee, leaving just enough room for her soymilk, she inhaled the deliciously addicting scent. Taking one more glance outside at the swirling flakes, she turned and left her kitchen.

Sasha strolled through the High Street house in the manner she often did, slowly allowing herself to take in the history of the home, dragging her fingertips softly along the crevices of the antique furniture. Images danced within her mind with daydreams of how good her home would smell it were full of daisies - her favorite flower - and how Charles and Eliza may have spent a morning together like this. Maybe Eliza would be writing to her grandmother, whom Sasha discovered lived in England. Or maybe Charles would be keeping the books on the pub. Would their little girl be playing with the baby doll and wooden toy crib that Sasha had found in the attic? Would Jakob, Eliza's brother, be teaching his nephew how to properly make a snow person outside? Perhaps engaging into a snowball fight, the way she and her friends had done?

As Sasha stood in front of the stained glass window, so beautifully original to the house, she took comfort in the thought that perhaps Charles and Eliza had indeed spent their snowy days just as she imagined it in her daydreams. Snowflakes glistening in the trees

123

added prismatic bouncing light beams throughout her parlor, making the room feel extra happy.

Winding her way up the stairs to the upper floor, while Henry was still blissfully asleep, she placed her now empty holiday mug on the table next to the attic door, and ascended up the steep, narrow staircase. *Can't believe I was scared of spiders the first time I came up here*, Sasha mused. That day seemed to be forever ago, now.

Normally, after one of her memory-like dreams, there would be a particular item she would be in search of. Today, there was no goal in mind of a wish list item, other than the key to the trunk. Unlocking the 1904 World Fair traveling trunk was always a priority for Sasha. *But the key will show itself when it wants to be found*, she concluded.

Moving over to the only set of windows in the wooden room, Sasha peered out to the snowy day to see not a single person was out on this New Year's Day yet. The pure white snow covered mass on the streets lay undisturbed, coating the picturesque town in a blanket of white crystals gleaming in trees from the sun. As she turned, Sasha noticed some faded carvings on the edge of the wood, under the windowsill. *Score tallies?*

And as though she were watching down on the

scene itself, she envisioned a daydream - or a memory - right there at the window. Charles and Andrew were with two other gentlemen, seated at a card table gambling their morning away. More specifically, the fellas were playing poker, she realized as she took in the money splashed across the table, next to brandy and cigars. Gambling appeared to be a favored past time for the gentlemen. Through her mind's eye she watched as Andrew leaned over to the window, and Sasha could faintly hear the unknown man on Charles' right asking if everything was okay. Andrew replied, telling him he was just keeping a look out as he called the bet, laying his down four queens with a smirk. As he scooped up the pile of money, Charles etched the win into the wall.

The scene faded from her mind, and Sasha shook herself as though she were dizzy. Had gambling been illegal on residential premises? It sure appeared to her that it had been.

- - -

Henry found Sasha sitting on the ground with heaps of letters and newspaper clippings strewn about the floor around her, empty hat boxes encircling those piles, and a small leather-bound book in her hands. Hanks came up the stairs after him and settled into her lap in a comforting manner. The fluffy male cat hated it when Sasha was upset.

Sasha's eyes popped up, tear-stricken, and met his ice blue eyes that were heavily concerned. "They weren't together forever!" Her voice was unsteady and filled with unequivocal sadness. "Eliza, she left... she left this place and everything with it, behind."

Sasha looked at Henry, and felt as though her own heart had been broken, smashed into a million pieces that no longer fit together. *Pieces that are no longer in accordance*, Sasha realized. *If I feel like this, what must have Eliza felt?* Sasha felt a fresh wave of oncoming tears with that thought. With her heart busting at every seam, she realized just how much she wanted her grandmother then, and cried even harder.

Henry sat next to her on the dusty wooden floor and picked up a letter addressed to Mrs. Elijah Williams, the handwriting in the most elegant script he'd ever seen. "What did this letter tell you?"

"Eliza sent this journal to her mother," Sasha held the brown leather book in front of her. Golden initials decorated the cover. "She asked that it be placed with her trunk, which should be kept in the attic. Then Eliza requested the home be put up for sale, saying she would never return." Sasha sniffled. "It's written here, in the letter, that her once precious memories were just too much to handle. Eliza must've felt incredible pain to leave her life here." Sasha retrieved the letter from Henry's hands. "This letter appears to only have been read once."

Henry now seemed even more puzzled than when he had found her sitting there in her mess of tears. "Once was probably enough," he said firmly. "And everything is up here. They must have known she wouldn't return. Her mother, Mrs. Williams, must've taken her word very seriously." He looked at all of the letters circled around them. "What broke them up?"

Sasha shook her head and pathetically slouched her shoulders, "I don't know. I've been reading the diary, but some of it's been faded."

"If you don't know, why are you crying?"

"Because!" A fresh tear fell into the dust, "the way Eliza described her love for him, and Charles of her, it's heartbreaking – absolutely heartbreaking – that they didn't grow old together. These two beings were made for each other like two halves of a puzzle." Slamming the book shut, Sasha blinked at him with her watery and sad chocolate eyes. *If their love story couldn't survive, what hope is their for us*, Sasha gloomily thought.

"I think you and Alice should give this a rest." Henry reached for the journal, "This is not our story, and I don't care to see you so upset like this." Henry touched her cheek and drew her in more for a kiss. Her pale rosy lips were salty from her tears and the kiss wasn't a deep, stimulating type of kiss. No, it was the kind of kiss that simply said, 'I'm here for you. I'm not going anywhere.' This was the type kind of kiss that scared her.

Sasha felt her confidence, so newly developed, crawl into a cave. She no longer felt brave in her relationship or life. Learning of Eliza's fate rocked Sasha to her very core. What if Alice was right - and Sasha was reincarnated - then what was her story about to become?

chapter fourteen.

Daisies, nothing but daisies. No further bloom must be in existence in their small town other than fresh cut white, yellow or lavender daises. Eliza's birthday was today and Charles was flabbergasted by the grand receiving line of flowers the entire town gifted his wife annually, with bouquets ascending the front porch steps of their Victorian home that crossed through the front doors in a steady fragrant river. As far as he wished, the flowers would have been sent to the Judge's Manor, where the ball in celebrations of Eliza's birthday was to be held that very evening.

The heightened scent of the perfumed plant provided him a hefty headache, and just as Charles placed a hand on the screen door, prepared to freshen his senses with air that smelled of newly cut spring grass, the sound of wheels skidding across the hardwood floors halted Charles midway through the door. Several thuds later, accommodated with the groan of a four-year-old, forced him to turn back into the house.

"Austen." Charles retraced his steps back into the parlor, only to discover scratches on the floor creating a path straight to his son, who was struggling to stand up on his roller skates once more. Austen was the first-born son of his and Eliza's ever growing family, and looked very much like his mother. Except for his son's big brown eyes were constantly filled with curiosity, a trait he took in from his favorite Uncle. And, at the moment, his child was covered head-to-toe in dirt and blooms. Charles could've helped his young son, but instead he let out a deep laugh at the sight before him. "As your mother would say, son, you take right after your Uncle Jakob."

"Well, so what if he does?" Jakob – quite grown up since Charles first met him so many years ago in Scottie's Pub – rolled into the room on his own pair of skates, carrying yet another delivery of lavender daisies into the room. "At least, since we have a never-ending receiving line of Mother Earth's blooms, this mess will be easily replaced."

"Are you sure, the two biggest magnets for trouble I know, aren't just bowling for daisies?" Charles tried not to grin at his son, appearing as serious as he could manage.

"No, but thanks for the idea, old man." Jakob winked, slapping Charles shoulder as he leaned over to help Austen up. Charles just shook his head, knowing it was useless with this happy-go-lucky uncle and nephew. Letting out one last chuckle, he continued with the plan of stepping outside.

Out on the porch, a small, delicate giggle could be heard. He followed the sound to his right, around the small bend of the wrap-around porch. It was there, under the shade of the large pine tree, where his wife was gently rocking their daughter Alma Jane - the giggling culprit - on her lap.

Eliza tilted her chin up towards his enchanted blue eyes, dazzling him with an amount of incandescent happiness behind her smile that squeezed his heart. Around her neck was the shiny gold locket Charles gifted her for her birthday. The memory of waking her up with the gift hugged his soul.

"I take it by the excessive noise and hearty laughter that Jakob is up to no good?" The grin on her face left out any doubt that she minded the mess much.

"Please, my dear, don't forget about our angelic son Austen." Charles leaned forward, kissing his wife on the forehead as he swooped up his precious baby girl, a

131

mirror image of his wife. Well, except for her pale blue eyes. Charles twirled her around, up and down, and then cradled the sweet cooing child in his protective arms. "Promise me your looks come with your mother's coordination and grace little one."

Alma Jane giggled again, smiling at her father as though she was almost in complete agreement with him.

- - -

"Rumors are swirling about the town that it is the baker's wife who has been creating those delectable sweets. And that the baker himself cannot even manage a boil of water on the stove! Can you imagine?"

The whole town seemed to be in attendance of the birthday ball at the Judge's Manor. Charles and Eliza stood amongst their friends, Andrew and Annabelle, as friends tend to do, as they discussed the town gossip.

"I hope Mr. Thomas Pratt does not receive wind of this news. I could not bear to watch her be beaten by his verbally abusive mouth and foul titles." Eliza had never forgotten the first and only impression gluttonous drunk man had left on her. "Further more, what does it matter if she is behind those wonderfully decadent treats? What should it matter if she's a woman? Every man, to my knowledge, has a better woman standing off to the side, pulling the strings."

Andrew fawned a sigh of desperation. "Alas, she has us gentlemen all figured out. What *will* we do?" His face was full of pretend panic with the twitches of a smile.

"I think Eliza's on to something."

"Well of course you do, my darling Annabelle," Andrew said, "You're the half pulling the strings!"

The friends laughed with their playful banter. To Charles, when with friends, one was with family. "So the fair is almost here," he said to change the subject away from town gossip.

"Take me to Saint Louis, Charles?" Andrew questioned with his joshing face. With his hands clasped together, the very large man batted his eyelashes at his ginger-haired friend.

"Well, only if you promise to buy me extravagantly shiny trinkets, Andrew."

Andrew, with a frown marring his charming face, exclaimed, "Do none of you care for the Louisiana Purchase Exposition? This is a historical moment!"

Ignoring Andrew, Charles wife turned towards her dearest friend. "Annabelle, do you know the type of souvenirs that will be sold there?" Eliza was now serious, as a woman who clearly had excellent taste,

133

and had a twinkle in her eye at the idea of shopping.

"Oh no! No more decorating our home Eliza," Charles stated. She poked him in the ribs, and resumed discussing jewels and trinkets with Annabelle.

Charles gambled on racing horses with a slower start at the gate than these women and their shopping habits. Taking a glance at Andrew, Charles the noted the man appeared to be in physical pain from the amount of money he was going to lose due to Annabelle's love of trinkets. Not that the man would ever tell his wife 'No'. That would be a very difficult thing for Andrew. He looked at Eliza, seeing she was equally as excited about the fair, which only made him feel more contentment in his ever-swelling heart. Eliza lived with ease about her manners, a true joy for life, and laughter that Charles swore could end wars.

"Annabelle, we should look for a sapphire for you. The jewel is the exact shade of your eyes."

- - -

In fact, sapphires are exactly what the women found. Charles was hard pressed to say if there were anything those vicious, pretty-eyed shoppers did not find. Charles began to regret bringing his pocketbook. The whole family joined in for the excursion that day. The 1904 World's Fair was an once-in-a-lifetime kind of experience. A memory made right in their own backyard. Saint Louis was a star on the world map, and everybody was there to witness the historical moment.

"A delectable waffle cone for ice cream? Why has no one created this scrumptious treat before?"

Jakob had seen the Fair in its entirety, and they only thing he took interest in was a brand new conception for his favorite sweet treat. Literally, the young man ate his whole way through the day. Little Austen was not far behind, the small boy trying to shadow his favored uncle as much as possible, until Eliza told him he'd be off to bed early if he didn't stop trying to ruin his gut within one singular day. The two youthful parents were amazed neither one was ill yet.

A photography booth grabbed Eliza's attention away from a dressmaker, much to his relief.

"Charles, let us take a photograph? This day has to be remembered forever, exactly the way we are living it. One day, we'll want to recall this memory."

Eliza grinned happily at her husband, knowing she never had to ask her husband for permission, but doing so anyway. Together, they had more than most could dream of. Together, their souls were attuned to each other. Together, Charles and Eliza had a love that could last lifetimes. A photo would never really caption all that they had, but it would be nice to have, just the same.

Collectively with Andrew, Annabelle and their son Trent, Judge and Mrs. Williams, Jakob and his ice cream cone, Austen and Alma Jane, Charles and Eliza had several photos taken with souvenirs for their remembrance. Would someday, someone unknown come across their things? Know who they were?

Judge Williams purchased Mrs. Williams and his daughter matching trunks with the fair's emblem. The brown travel pieces were quite the exceptional finds with interiors of bold red lining, and a secret compartment for the key to be kept in. Only Eliza and her mother were told where the trap door was, so as only they could be the keepers of the secret.

Charles and Andrew bought their wives bejeweled decorative boxes with earrings hidden inside, a gift for later. Charles chose pristine pearls for Eliza, to compliment her love of gold threaded gowns, and Andrew selected sapphires for Annabelle that matched the exact blue of her jeweled-toned eyes. Austen stood proudly next to his mother for the picture, who was holding his baby sister, balancing in a new pair of roller skates.

The group picture, commemorating the day, was taken in front of The Pike. It was a beautiful setting, with the nearly mile-long carnival behind them, illuminated with lights and marvelous creations. Charles knew that this memory was certainly worthy of remembrance. In a way, it was just one more perfect day with Eliza. He was not sure he would ever get his fill of them, for he treasured his wife and family, as they were his world – his everything.

chapter fifteen.

In the passing weeks, Sasha hadn't touched the diary because she was fearful to discover what happened between Charles and Eliza that catapulted her into such loathsome pain. A very rainy spring season followed the brutal winter that year, which was leaving Sasha cooped up inside. But on this particular storm-ridden day, she was alone in her house, and something within her was tugging at her string of curiosity. She needed a break from writing her book, a love story that Grace talked her through from time to time at the corner coffee shop. Henry would be going straight from the courthouse to his restaurant, and Sasha wouldn't be seeing him today until she met Alice for dinner later that night. The day was hers in its entirety.

Maybe it was the coolness of the spring storm, or

the spell of the flashing lightning, but the idea to begin reading Eliza's journal again was stronger than ever, and her curiosity was winning over her will power. Hidden among other books in her library, which was where she was standing now, was the ending to a story she had become so utterly connected with. She wanted to read it, she really did. But Sasha knew that she wasn't looking at the happiest of endings.

Resigning herself to the idea that fate and coincidence perhaps was the same thing, Sasha still did not agree with Alice that she was the reincarnated Eliza. Because if she did believe in that possibility, Sasha was bound and determined to do everything possible to avoid Eliza's heartbreak. No, Sasha was simply the person who would learn of the story and perhaps share with someone – someday – of the greatest love story and tragedy she ever knew. After all, wasn't it better to have love and lost, rather to never have loved at all? *And exactly at what point did I, Sasha Reed, turn into such a romantic sap?*

Grabbing the brown leather bound book, Sasha moved into her parlor, curled up in a chair by the second stained glass window in the home that was being pelted by raindrops. Taking a deep, calming breath, she fanned through the pages until she was almost of the end of Eliza's journal. There, she discovered that something was stuck in the fold of the page. It was a newspaper clipping, an obituary, for

Charles Theodore Hoffmeister, age 44. A deep unease settled into the pit of her stomach.

As she read over it, it mentioned nothing of specifically how Eliza's beloved husband had passed away, instead declaring only that there was an accident on May 1st, 1905. Charles left behind a widow and a toddler daughter, and his place of propriety was to be sold to the bank. The disturbing obituary clipping referenced nothing of Eliza's name, or of any other ties to the community.

The last line read,

> **"He shall be remembered always, laid to his final resting place by those who loved, respected and cherished him as a husband, father and friend. His soul shall be honored, as will his memory, for as long as time goes on."**

As she picked up the excerpt to flip it over, two dried and pressed white roses fell out of the next page, joined by another clipping. It was a second obituary.

Sasha gasped at the name and age: Charles Austen Hoffmeister, age 8. The pit in her stomach crashed through to the floor. Not only had Charles died, but also so had their eldest child, Austen. Sasha would wager a large sum that it'd been the same accident to kill both father and son – likely the same instantaneous moment that both bright lights fell from the Earth.

Sasha in-took a sharp breath. They hadn't fallen out of love or broken up, as she'd so easily believed in her earlier conclusion from New Years Day. Charles and Austen had died – tragically – and Eliza ran from the pain of losing them. Eliza had run from what Sasha feared the most, a broken heart.

- - -

Later that night, Sasha could feel Henry's eyes on her from the bar, well aware he'd been silently worried about her for months. Henry knew her history, and that she only had one foot in when it came to their relationship. Having confided in him that theirs was her first real relationship, Sasha was trying so hard to not let her fears run her life for her anymore. And that was true – she *was* trying to let down every wall with him. Sasha knew she might even be falling for him, though she was unsure of just how much. But if Charles and Eliza had taught her anything, it was that all good things come to an end. It was a fear that was difficult for her to ignore, and was a constant reminder hanging in the back of her mind.

Alice breezed through the door, her blonde chin length pixie-cut hair sprinkled with a few raindrops that her umbrella didn't catch. Plopping down in the chair on the left side of Eliza, with her back to the rain her friend mused, "Mother nature's been crying an awful lot this spring."

Simply put, that was Alice. The girl had a precariously poetic way with her words. Her sapphire eyes sparkled with the untold humor she found in her whimsical statement.

"Alice, Charles and Eliza didn't make it." Sasha wasn't sure, but she thought Alice's brightness dulled a little, just a pinch or two. *Wow, blurt much?*

"What do you mean?" Alice asked her cautiously, as though she was approaching a frightened kitten.

"Well, I thought they just broke up, and I hadn't wanted to tell you until I knew why..."

"Broken up? Charles and Eliza? The most romantic couple of our town's existence?"

"I know, I know. I was wrong thou--."

"I knew it! There's no way they couldn't have ended anything as strong as their bond. From everything we know, their love was eternal."

"It did end in heartbreak, Alice. Charles died in an accident, along with their son, Austen. And then she left... she left because she couldn't take the pain. Eliza moved back to England to live with her grandmother. She and her daughter, Alma Jane, never returned. Everything was left behind. She sent a journal back, and had her mother store it in the attic – my attic."

Like a light bulb burning out, Alice's brightness definitely dulled then. She reminded Sasha of a kid who just found out fairytale characters weren't real. Those were just fables for children to believe in, stories that gave the youth in the world a reason to believe in magic. Maybe that was what the story of Charles and Eliza meant to Alice, a reason to believe in fate.

"Alice.."

As if her friend had read her mind, she exclaimed, "It's still fate, Sasha."

Their conversation paused as Henry brought them the drinks that they never bothered to order. As she watched him walk out of earshot, Alice continued, "I think *you* are meant to finish their story. You and Henry will have the happy ending they never got."

Sasha shook her head. Alice and fate, it *was* her fairytale story. "This is not fate, Alice. Maybe this is all a coincidence, a fluke, a chance of luck. But, I'm not the reincarnated or born-again Eliza. I'm just the girl who ran away from her own pain of her grandmother – my only family – dying."

Sasha paused to take a sip of her cocktail. The similarity of her and Eliza both running away from their lives was not lost on her, but she wasn't going to point that out to Alice either. "However, I am going to do something for Charles and Eliza. I'm going to tell their story to the world. Eliza left her diary detailing their entire love tale, start to finish."

"Maybe that's fate then," Alice offered. "Maybe that's why you are here."

Sasha shrugged, tired of telling Alice it wasn't fate and just tried to show her indifference to it.

Alice frowned, "there is one thing I'm wondering though."

"What?"

"Why would your grandmother have had that photo of the High Street house in her trunk? She couldn't have known about Charles and Eliza, but yet it was that particular photo that enticed you to move here."

Sasha couldn't answer that. She, too, had pondered again and again over the same question. *The matching trunk? The photo of the house? Where had it all come from?* She had no idea, but that she knew writing about Charles and Eliza was something she *had* to do, and Sasha would discover the how's and the why's of the reasons everything connected. Again, this could all be a coincidence, as she had no sound idea of where her grandmother had picked up the brown clunky piece of storage. Was the trunk in the attic originally Eliza's or Mrs. Williams? How had one gotten to New York, and one remained with the house after all this time, completely undisturbed by time?

chapter sixteen.

May Day. The first day of May. In many countries, this was a day of joyful jubilee and celebration. For Sasha, it was a day of poignant gloominess and remembrance, for she now knew of three people who had died on May Day. Her grandmother had been cremated, and Sasha now sat under the bridge after having laid her to her final resting place in the river, alongside the train tracks. Sasha struggled so deeply one year ago with saying goodbye to her grandmother, and now, she felt like she was finally ready. The beauty of spreading her ashes into the river – to Sasha – was that her spirit would never be still, it would continue to flow throughout the world, current by current, dancing in the wind. The thought brought a small smile to her eyes, as Sasha knew her grandmother would love to dance in the wind.

Sasha sighed as she placed the urn back into her bag, and pulled out a delicate note card. Addressing it to Henry, she opened the card to write, but then paused as she glanced over to the children playing on a nearby playground. The sound of their joyful laughter swirled into air.

She watched as a little boy pushed his sister on a merry-go-round. The older boy ran in conjunction with it, around and around, until the speed was finally at the pace where he wanted it, and jumped aboard with his sister. The boy smiled proudly in his accomplishment. *Kids so innocent,* she thought. *They live to smile and laugh, as much as they possibly can.* She wondered, as she watched them in idle curiosity, paying no attention to the train whistles in the distance.

Sasha supposed it was children who really lived their lives to the fullest, day in and day out. Eventually, when you became an adult, you just started living to get through the day. When does that change occur? When did it within her? Was it instantaneous? Slowly over time? Jealously momentarily touched her when Sasha realized she wanted to live her life to its fullest, day in and day out. Relief washed over her when Sasha felt her walls begin to crumble entirely.

Seeing Henry walking towards her, she mused at how he always knew where to find her. In his hands was a bouquet of sun-colored daisies, tied together with a matching yellow ribbon. Yellow had been her grandmother's favorite color, and she knew then, that he brought them to lay in the water. Henry had brought flowers for her grandmother. She felt a tug in chest, and a slow warmth creep through her body. Focusing on the small note in the card, in the most elegantly script she could manage, Sasha wrote a simple sentence, then, to the man that introduced her to a whole new realm of insights and possibilities. Closing the card, she reached for its envelope when a little girl's scream ripped through her serenity.

With the card in her hand, Sasha hurriedly lunged towards the tracks, her movement halted only by the steepness of the place under the bridge where all her stuff remained. As quickly as she could she ran towards the merry-go-round, and saw Henry was running too.

The young boy, who just a minute earlier had been so proud of his playground accomplishment with her little sister, had somehow managed to wedge his tiny foot into the tracks, and the train that had been whistling just in the background rounded the corner. There was no denying it was full steam ahead, coming towards them, with the distance closing all too quickly.

Henry reached the boy first, having been closer in range. The child was freaking out, trying with all his anxious might to free his foot loose from the railroad tracks. When Henry joined the tug of war with his ankle,

Sasha slowed her a halt without realizing her own movements. She could no longer hear the train, or the little girls screaming pleas for help. Faintly, Sasha could see a train, but was barely able to breathe in even a gasp of air. *Was she even moving?*

Before her was Eliza, standing in front of her, screaming for help and hysterical. Tears were rolling down her cheeks and footsteps were running behind her. It was Austen wedged into the train tracks, with Jakob and Charles yanking on the boy's leg. There was a baby crying. How was she seeing this scene?

Sasha felt hollow and numb as she watched before her, unable to move as she stood frozen in time, rooted to a sensation of doom she had never knew before.

Henry. Charles. Henry. Charles.

This was it. This was the accident and it was repeating itself. Was this fate? Could it be so cruel? *Henry.*

Screw fate, Sasha cursed. Unfrozen with that though, she felt her feet move forward again, straight though where Eliza was standing, and gasped as the coal train whooshed passed her at an incredible speed.

Stumbling back, Sasha screamed and screamed for Henry to answer her without any response. When the train car was gone, after what felt like days had passed, she cried out. "No…!" Sasha wasn't sure if she made any noise at all, as hot tears spilled out of her sorrowed chocolate eyes, and she dropped to her knees.

The card that was somehow still in her hand fluttered to the ground. Landing open, the simple but powerful note Sasha had written to Henry was visible. In an elegant, familiar scribble were the words *"I Love You"*. She loved Henry.

chapter seventeen.

Sasha sat on the floor of her bedroom, cross-legged with Hanks on her lap, rifling through her grandmother's trunk. It was this trunk that encouraged her to move to the small town and buy this house – her house. *Had it only been a year ago?* Her grandmother had basically been the cause of her discovering Charles and Eliza, Alice and Luke, Grace and... *Henry*.

Sasha sighed, and began placing the items back into the trunk. Maybe it was just the light, but Sasha thought she noticed a small lump in the lining of the lid. Sliding her hand along the inner red lining of the corner of the lid, she felt the snag in the fabric. There was a small hole, just big enough to fit two of her fingers to reach in and touch something. *Paper, maybe?* Pulling on the item, she wrenched it out of the small tear, realizing it was a letter... from her grandmother?

Curiosity sprang forth and she ripped in open:

To My Dearest Sasha,

By now, I'm quite sure you have found the photograph of an old Queen Anne Victorian house. I'm also sure that you have since acquired more than one question about the photograph and why I've kept it so many years.

I bought this trunk from an antique house in the city some twenty years ago. Perhaps, I mentioned once before that my mother once told me she'd been at the 1904 World's Fair in St. Louis? If not, well, please know I thought the item to be somewhat nostalgic at the time. The man who sold it to me stated that this trunk had a sister to it - an identical twin trunk. Though I thought he was just trying to make a sale at the time, and fibbing a story, it was years later when I realized he was correct.

Imagine my surprise when I found a snag of loosened fabric in the lining, much as you did to find this letter, and discovered a

154

photograph was placed inside the pocket of space. How interesting, I thought, that a person would go through all of the trouble of creating such a hiding place for an old picture. Although, now that I think of it, for the original owner of the trunk the photo was probably new at the time, and perhaps quite a special memory.

Though I tried to research the house in the photo, I never had much luck. I never found the story behind the address, and I'm afraid I lost the urge to follow it through. I kept the photograph with the trunk because, to me, what was found together should stay together. I have always believed in the idea of a tale to be told, a trait you have since acquired.

Along the inside of the lock, you will also find a tiny lever that opens a secret compartment. I never found the answer to what I discovered inside.

Follow your heart Sasha, and life will show you the path.

I Love You.

Your Grandmother.

Sasha closed the letter and held it to her chest, sighing in the happiness at receiving one more "*I Love You*" from her grandmother. Had her grandmother had known she would run from the pain? Is that why she left her the trunk — to give her a place to run to? Grandmother had been so sure of herself that she knew Sasha would find the photograph? If anybody knew her, it was her grandmother.

Sasha placed the letter back where she found it, since that was where it was meant to be for now, and traced her hand along the inside of the lock. There, her fingertips brushed against a tiny piece of metal that nobody would ever suspect. Pushing on it until it moving into the trunk wall like a button, she heard a popping noise. Not seeing anything new inside the interior of the trunk, she felt confused.

It wasn't until she glanced around the trunk to its left side that Sasha saw a tiny flap open along the bottom of the trunk, near the back corner. Yanking it towards her, she discovered a tiny compartment with enough room in it for her cell phone. Of course, a cell phone wasn't what she discovered.

Inside the secret compartment were two things: a golden locket and a skeleton key. *A key!* Quickly she pulled the key out of its hiding space and stuck it in the pocket of her jeans. Retrieving the necklace, she held the chain up to the sunlight streaming in from the windows. Sasha noticed a small heart engraved on it. Since the chain was long enough she could slip it over her head and around her neck, so she did just that. It took a little effort, but she managed to pry it open, finding a faded photo of Charles on one side and Eliza on the other. *How did these two things end up in this trunk, if Eliza's trunk is upstairs?*

Opening the attic door, Hanks once again rushed his way up in front of Sasha. Finding the trunk again, she pulled the heavy box in front of the only two windows in the room. In the light she could see that it was indeed an exact replica of her grandmother's. *The sister trunk!*

Taking the old, clunky skeleton key from her pocket, Sasha thrust it into the rusty lock, having to jiggle it slightly. Closing her eyes and wishing her heart's desire, she turned the key and heard a click.

Her eyes fluttered open in amazement. What would she find? Lifting the lid, she saw a golden-stitched wedding gown fit for a queen. Retrieving the dress from the clashing red lining of the antique trunk, Sasha twirled in front of the windows with it. She had never seen a more exquisite gown in all her life. Thoughtfully, Sasha proceeded to place the dress on the old mannequin figure she had bumped into the first day she had explored the attic.

Going back to the trunk, she continued her search,

finding an old doll, a white Baptism baby gown, a pair of beat up roller skates, blue prints to the house, and the matching jeweled box to the one she had placed on her mantle in the parlor. Steadying herself, Sasha opened the decorative box, finding inside it two wedding bands, gold and simple. The smaller one had hearts engraved on the exterior of the band, and the phrase *'In Accordance To The Heart'* on the inside of the ring. Sasha realized it matched the golden locket necklace she found in the other trunk. Returning the dazzling box back into the trunk, Sasha then felt for the hidden lever, and opened this trunk's special hidden compartment.

Moving to the left side of the trunk, Sasha found another letter. The parchment appeared to be much older, and was addressed to no one in particular:

To Whom It May Concern:

This trunk contains the most precious memories of my daughter's lifetime. It is at her request that these memories stay where they were born, in the home her cherished husband built for her. It is with a deep, heavy sorrow that the life she knew here ended so soon.

Elizabeth Alma Williams Hoffmeister loved every person whom she ever befriended unconditionally. Her love was

so great it could last through lifetimes.

Sincerely,
Mrs. Elijah Williams

That's it? That's all the explanation Sasha was going to get? This trunk had never been Eliza's, but rather it was Mrs. Williams. That must mean her grandmother's trunk had been Eliza's. How had the piece ended up in New York? Had she left it there on her way to England? *What a small world.*

Sasha placed the disappointing letter back in its hiding place, and shut the hidden compartment. Standing up and brushing the dust off of her, she turned as she heard footsteps ascending the narrow attic stairs.

"Hey, are you ready? The barbecue is pretty much ready and good to go." Luke had the sparkle of a child sometimes, always ready for a laugh and some fun. "And I'm hungry." *And always with an appetite*, she mused.

"Yeah – yes – I'm ready. Sorry," she tried to look apologetic, "I got distracted." Sasha bent over to pick up something from the trunk, then shut the year-long mystery, moving it out of the sunlight and pushing it back into hiding. "Let's go!" she said, following Luke outside down the stairs and outside to her backyard.

It had been a month since the train accident, and

Alice had convinced her that a barbecue would be a great idea. The vegetarian girl – who didn't own a grill – was hosting a barbecue. The irony was not lost on Sasha. So for the first, and likely the last time in her life, she went out and bought a grill. Then, much to his chagrin, Luke put the thing together.

Standing outside on her back patio, she pictured the first time she had let her guard down with Henry. For a moment she saw twinkling lights and stars, and smiled at the memory.

"What are you smiling at?"

"At what I found in the attic," Sasha said coyly.

"And what's that?"

Sasha looked into those crystal blue eyes and let herself giggle, just a little bit. "I found blue prints to the house."

Henry frowned, "what's so special about that?"

"Take a look at them."

Henry laid out the blue prints on the table, though it was a bit challenging with one arm in a black sling because of the torn muscle in his shoulder and the white cast around his wrist. Nobody had died on May Day, but it had been a close call and Sasha couldn't even begin to think about it. Not yet.

160

As Sasha held down one side of the blue prints, Alice bounded up to the table with her curly blonde hair bouncing, to hold down the other end. Sasha supposed she would have to tell Alice that her finding the old photograph, and picking up her life to move to the small Missouri town, hadn't been fate at all. It was, after all, just pure dumb luck that her grandmother purchased a trunk that reminded her of a tale her mother had once told her. And the fact that she and her new friends looked so much like somebody else in the past was also a coincidence. People look alike all the time. *Don't they?*

Henry sucked in a breath, looking up from the table in awe. Sasha smiled as his eyes widened with the realization of a new undisclosed mystery the house was holding.

"There's a secret passageway."

Alice let go of the paper, giddy with glee as it rolled back to Sasha's hand. "Let's go find it!"

Luke, who had been silently grilling oversized mushrooms the whole time Henry reviewed the blue prints, finally interjected, "Can't we wait until tomorrow to start a new adventure? I'd rather eat first."

Sasha laughed. The four of them could wait until tomorrow. After all, she found a story to tell... her own.

epilogue.

Willow James was sitting in front of a man who was maybe in his mid-fifties, completely bald on the top of his head, but still had a few tufts of hair around the rim of his head. It was mostly gray and matched the caterpillar mustache that was framing his lips. Lips which were not frowning – or smiling – but were pursed in a question instead.

"Ms. James, before I tell you if we can or can't publish your book, I would like to ask you why it should be printed for the world to read. Why is *this* the story you wrote?"

Willow smiled as her chin-length hair – curly, dark

brown and perfectly disheveled – fell slightly over her face. Her velvety brown eyes twinkled with delight.

"This is a story that has to be told, Mr. Parker. This is the story that constantly questions the meanings of fate or coincidence? Are we meant to be with someone? Is there only one true love in the world for us? Are soul mates real? And for that matter, is love real? Does it exist?"

Mr. Parked had chubby, rosy cheeks. It reminded Willow of her grandfather.

"And does it?" the man inquired.

"While I sit here, still as uncertain as ever, Sasha would say yes. Sasha would say yes, because she found love. She found fate – even if she doesn't realize it. Or at the very least, Sasha will never admit to it."

The portly man leaned back in his chair, thoughtfully pursing his lips again. As the publisher clasped his hands together in a prayer like manner, resting first on her manuscript and then against his chin, Willow held her breath in suspense.

Mr. Parker breathed in, looked at Willow in her eyes and said, "Prince's House of Publishing would love to print your book. Let's set up a meeting with marketing and an editor for the end of the week." He stood and walked around his desk, holding his hand out to her.

Willow stood and delightfully giggled. Taking his hand into hers, she pulled him into a hug. "Thank you Mr. Parker, thank you so much!"

Saying goodbyes, she turned to walk out the door, to where she would pass cubicle after cubicle until she reached the elevator, with a triumphant stride and bounce in her step.

If this were a movie, she thought, *there would be a song playing right about now, about a lifetime that lasted one hundred years.* Imagining the soundtrack to her life, and to her stories, was what helped Willow get through writer's block.

As Willow James stepped into the elevator, she looked at the person standing next to her. Before her was a tall ginger-haired man with the bluest of eyes, and Willow smiled once more, just as the elevator doors closed.

the end.

about the author.

Boonville, Missouri born and raised, Liz Rau now resides in Colorado. As an avid and passionate supporter of the performance arts community, Liz's background and hobbies include dance, choreography, theatre and writing.

With a Bachelor of Science degree in Mass Communications from Southeast Missouri State University, Liz continues her education in communications while currently employed in the sales field; and actively travels throughout the world to the places that inspire her.

With six nieces and nephews, she often considers her role as an "Auntie" as one of her greatest pleasures in life. She also dotes on her two cats, one of which is black & fluffy...perhaps the real-life inspiration for Hanks?

Liz also find inspiration through Judy Garland movies, Christmas lights, music, rainy days, daydreams, and of course, good old fashioned people watching.

acknowledgements.

Thank you to my parents. Not only did you give me a wonderful childhood that has inspired many stories, like *Pieces*, you've helped tremendously with the execution of my creative process. Mom, thank you for being the first to read every book. Dad, thank you for being an excellent book manager;)

To Mat, owner of Blue Bamboo Creative, your design talents are incredible! This book cover is AMAZING! You're one-of-a-kind sir!

To Lindsey, I borrowed your daughter's name. I hope you don't mind...

To Candace Viertel, Gordon Jewelers, Cheryl Rudauskas and Travel Leaders Parker: thank you for your encouragement, friendship, and for hosting book signings for me. Thank you SO much!

Candace. Thank you for proof reading *Pieces* in the final hour!

Max, thank you for helping me with formatting issues when I'd rather have a meltdown from my frustrations with technology.

Thank you to all of my friends who have shared, downloaded, and spread my book(s) all over the world. Your kindness makes me smile.

Many thanks to everybody who has sent me a photo with their book. So far, it looks like my stories go great with a cup of coffee. Keep sending them folks! I love it!

notes from liz.

As I sit here, pondering exactly what to write, I am thinking about my family and my childhood. Life is funny, isn't it? When you're a kid growing up in a small town, you simply can't *wait* to get out of it. But now? Reflecting back on my life, I realize I draw so much inspiration from that small town life. My hometown is exactly what inspired this book.

My creativity sparks from the fact my parents encouraged my ability to use my imagination. I've never lost my passion to create stories, to daydream in the clouds, or sometimes think, "What if this had happened instead?" It's in those moments that a story can be born. Following it through is the hard part.

I challenge you to review your life, both in present and past, and to learn who you are in this world. After that, I challenge you to aspire to your dreams. After all, there's no reason to wait until tomorrow, is there?

fun facts.

- This story is set in Boonville, Missouri.

- I grew up in the house "just over on High Street". The house really was built by a saloon owner in 1893 named Charles Hoffmeister. However, I have no idea what his story is after that.

- A carriage stepping block belonging to Charles Hoffmeister still resides with the home. However, it is no longer located by the street, to ease the convenience of entering/exiting a carriage. The block, with the engraving of "C Hoffmeister" has been moved to the backyard.

- There really was a Judge Williams circa 1880-1961 in Boonville, Missouri.

- Boone's Opera Hall was inspired by Thespian Hall, which is a real working theatre, and I've always drawn inspiration from this place.

- The character of Annabelle Cooper was originally named Sarah. I changed the name after my good friend had her baby in August

2016. Cooper is the name of the county the town is located in.

- The character of Grace is named after a good friend from college. Her husband designed the book cover.

- This book was originally a short story I wrote in 2009 while I was bored at work one day. Good thing I don't work there anymore, or I'd likely be fired.

- Whenever I imagine chapter twelve, I hear the song "Carol of the Bells" in my mind.

- Tom Hanks is my favorite actor, and I've named a black cat after him in *Pieces of Accordance*, as well as the *Secrets, Spells and Tales* series.

- There isn't a Sloppy Jane's in Boonville, but there is a restaurant called WJ's. I recommend you go there for dinner when passing through town. The owner is also a lawyer.

- I once had a coworker who's maiden name was 'Hatfield'. I thought it sounded very old Hollywood and it's been in the story ever since.

- When I need to clear my mind, I listen to music. I love it all, but especially Britney Spears, Michael Buble, Nathan Lanier, Taylor Swift, Christina Grimmie, Ruth B., Grace, Priscilla Ahn, Kari Kimmel, Sleeping At Last, The Civil Wars and Toby Lightman.

- Henry is both a lawyer and a bartender in this story. This is because he's a combination of Eliza's father and husband in the past: Elijah Williams, a Judge, and Charles Hoffmeister, a saloon owner.

social media

Like me on Facebook, Twitter and Instagram to see behind the scenes of being an author! Plus, you may get sneak peeks at my next book!

Website: www.LizRauOfficial.com

Facebook – Liz Rau Official

Twitter – @LizRauOfficial

Instagram – @LizRauOfficial

Official Book Hashtag - #PiecesByRau

Please, please, please share fun photos of a Liz Rau book! Use the hashtag, and you just may end up on my Facebook page!

coming soon in 2017.

Spellbound: Secrets, Secrets, Spells and Tales

sneak a peek...

The Trials: Secrets, Secrets, Spells and Tales

CHAPTER ONE

Harry stood at the bow of The Craft and let out a deep sigh of despair as he watched the Salem coastline grow closer that morning. His first mate Callen shot him a sideways glance, the sigh taunting him to make a jab at Harry's expense. Harry chose to ignore the sarcastic look and kept his gaze straight. He knew what it was about. Harry hated going home - if he could even call it that. The Craft was his home and she wouldn't be sailing again anytime soon. Cold weather was about to set in and she was not a ship for winter floats in the chilly Atlantic. She'd barely come through that storm last night in one piece and it was going to take Harry the rest of the fall season before the repairs were done.

Callen had called Harry's callous and gruff mood days ago, telling the whole crew not to piss him off the day they docked, unless of course, they didn't want their jobs again come spring. "That ol' Irish temper ya know," he had said. "It can be a fiercer lashing than a fist."

Irish temper. Ha, what a laugh, Harry thought. Harry Ellison was a direct descendent of a Puritan Englishman named John Porter, Jr. The Porter family was notoriously associated to Salem from the fact they were directly linked to the infamous blemish on the town's history. A blemish that marked the Porter family heritage as well.

Now, over three hundred years later, Harry still felt the curse that had befallen the Porter family from those dangerous times where malicious gossip, a struggle for power, and a deep-rooted fear in the Devil himself eventually destroyed one of the first major ports for the East Indian Trade.

The reasons for The Trials have become misconstrued and ill-famed over the centuries with many forgetting what ignited the witch hunt. It all originally began with two households: the Putnam and the Porter families. The men of these families were sworn enemies with a long-standing rivalry, and it was a hateful battle for dominant control of the land and political leadership. It was a battle for power, Man's greatest weakness.

Ultimately, this struggle for power is what fueled The Trials, though that knowledge seemed all but forgotten these days. The brutality came to a head when the Porter men sabotaged fields harvested by the Putnam family, depleting the ability to maintain their crops that season. After that, the vicious war placed many in the village at odds, forcing them to choose a side.

The Putnam family, on the front of bringing morale to the community, brought the good and honorable Reverend Samuel Parris to the community. As a man of God and peace, surely calmness would blanket the village with his presence. Hope didn't remain long, however, as it was in the Reverend's home where the accusations of witchcraft and the accompanying afflictions first came to light. And though most people know the story of The Trials from there, very few have ever known of the black curse that was laid at the door of the Porter and Putnam families.

The Parris household had been home to a slave named Tituba and it was one of the Parris daughters who'd accused her of black arts and sorcery. Harry always assumed growing up and hearing these stories that Tituba was probably innocent and simply in the wrong place at the wrong time. He'd assumed she'd been an easy target. Harry's assumption couldn't have been further from the truth.

See, though Tituba was known to be a bit of a fortune-teller for the villagers in those days, it was later discovered that she was indeed the only real witch ever accused. She had even admitted those truths to the law during The Trials and claimed she only used occult knowledge to ward away evil. Somehow, Tituba was the only witch not executed during those times and the witch was banished back to her homeland.

Before Tituba left, however, she darkly cursed those who paved the path of her destruction. She hexed the families who lit the match that burned the fueled accusations. For eternity, the two instigating families would not know a home until their burden was buried and a bond was born. She was ruthless in the spell and every generation ultimately paid their dues.

The problem now was that Harry is the last known descendent of either family. Both of the families lost their respective prosperity and wealth, and neither had ever gained it back. Harry had somehow managed to accrue his own small fortune after years of hard work, but only time would tell if his luck would remain.

Strange accidents and deaths occurred on both sides of the ancestral trees throughout the many years and Harry knew those events had indeed been due to the curse, whether it was real or not. All a person had to do was believe and the destruction would be set in motion. As a child, Harry hadn't believed in these fairytales his grandfather would repeatedly refer to as sound reasoning, but as an adult, he now knew better.

Harry was acutely aware that after three hundred and twenty-four years, nothing had really changed. Hearsay and gossip still ruled the community, verily so. All one had to do was look at a news broadcast to see that all types of societies still appeared violently skeptical of any person whose beliefs and values differed from that of their own. He often wondered when history would begin to teach the present generations a new path of resolutions.

The whispers and judgment was why Harry's great-grandfather decided to change the family's last name to Ellison years ago. Hardly anybody in Salem could recall that Harry – Harold Tucker Ellison – was in fact, a Porter descendent.

The squawk of a seagull landing on the railing jarred Harry back to reality, causing him to recall Callen's Irish temper comment and he rolled his eyes again. It was the hair color that had people assuming he was of Irish descent. His scalp was thickly covered with flame colored ginger bristles, as was his five o'clock shadow of whiskers that were beginning to form a beard. He was grateful though, that people mistook him for Irish because he did indeed have a temper each time he made port in Salem's harbor. And as Callen liked to point out, it showed up just like clockwork.

Harry was unsure of how long he had actually been standing there, with his white-knuckle grasp on the railing, stewing about the fact he wouldn't be able to leave Salem again for a while, but his trance broke when he heard Callen's sharp intake of breath. He quizzically peered at him and then followed Callen's gaze to the shore, and his heart almost stopped when he found the subject of fascination, and his ocean-blue eyes widened in awe.

There on a balcony of a nearby residence, in the light of the pink-toned sunrise, stood a beautiful woman with wildly long raven hair. Harry was fairly sure there was no breeze, the surrounding trees weren't moving at all, yet her hair was blowing around her as if she was the one standing at the bow of a ship making port. And she was looking at them. The second that their eyes met Harry felt a connection. His arms quickly flushed with goose flesh and his mouth went dry, as though he had attempted to flirt and failed miserably – not that Harry experienced that scenario very often. And within him, somewhere deep and untouched, he felt a humming. *Why do I feel like I know her?*

He blinked and in a moment's time, the balcony was empty. *Had she even been there?* Harry wasn't entirely sure she was real to begin with. But then again, it wasn't likely possible for him and Callen to have the same hallucination, even in a town full of witches. Was it?

thank you:)

Made in the USA
San Bernardino, CA
27 March 2017